THEY CAME TO DODGE CITY

Burl Channing—In this wide-open town he had a job to do—track down a brutal killer and bring him to justice at any cost.

Emily Barker—A young widow torn between two strange men—one she has been taught to hate and one who has won her trust but will use her for his own savage gain.

Frank Killian—A dangerous man with a deck of cards, a deadly opponent when he's challenged.

Bat Masterson—Dodge was his town, and he could settle any argument with his gun.

HOOKED ON BOOKS
Used Books
1366 North Main St.
Walnut Creek, CA 94596
935-1025

$1.15

The Stagecoach Series

STATION I: DODGE CITY
STATION II: LAREDO

STAGECOACH STATION I:

DODGE CITY

Hank Mitchum

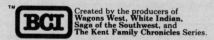

BCI Created by the producers of
Wagons West, White Indian,
Saga of the Southwest, and
The Kent Family Chronicles Series.

Executive Producer: Lyle Kenyon Engel

BANTAM BOOKS
TORONTO · NEW YORK · LONDON · SYDNEY

STAGECOACH STATION 1: DODGE CITY
A Bantam Book / October 1982

Produced by Book Creations, Inc.
Executive Producer: Lyle Kenyon Engel.

All rights reserved.
Copyright © 1982 by Book Creations, Inc.
Cover art copyright © 1982 by Bantam Books, Inc.
This book may not be reproduced in whole or in part, by
mimeograph or any other means, without permission.
For information address: Bantam Books, Inc.

ISBN 0-553-14752-8

Published simultaneously in the United States and Canada

Bantam Books are published by Bantam Books, Inc. Its trademark,
consisting of the words "Bantam Books" and the portrayal of a
rooster, is Registered in U.S. Patent and Trademark Office and in
other countries. Marca Registrada. Bantam Books, Inc., 666 Fifth
Avenue, New York, New York 10103.

PRINTED IN THE UNITED STATES OF AMERICA

O   0 9 8 7 6 5 4 3 2 1

STAGECOACH STATION I:

DODGE
CITY

Chapter 1

The old coach had the best of pedigrees for all the punishment time had dealt it. This was no mud wagon, obviously, but a genuine Concord from the New Hampshire works of Abbot & Downing—weighing a ton and a half, set on steel axles, the stout hickory body slung on heavy leather thoroughbraces. Standing scarred and battered here in thin spring sunlight amid the puddles of the wagon yard, it tempted a man to wonder at the thousands of miles it must have traveled, over how many rough Western roads and in what extremes of weather. Indian arrows must have bounced off its solid timbers; only strong suns and gritty desert winds could have scoured away its paint until the fancy clipper ship on either door panel was scarcely visible.

Well, these old Concords had been built to last. This one probably had a lot of miles in it yet.

Burl Channing walked up, carrying his hand grip and observing the man who was at work greasing the big wheel hubs. "This is the stage for Dodge City, I take it. When do we roll?"

The man cocked a look at him. "Be an hour, anyway," he grunted. "Maybe a mite longer if there's trouble siphoning Charlie out of that saloon across the street and pouring him into the driver's seat."

"He often give you that kind of trouble?"

"Well, Charlie Pitts hates horses, or so he claims. Sober, he can't even face the thought of them. But you put a few shots under his belt and the leathers in his hands and there ain't a better whip in the business."

Impatient at the thought of an hour to be killed, Channing left him and walked into the unpainted frame building that housed headquarters for the freight and stage line.

Here there were a few benches, piles of baggage, a banjo clock prominent on the station wall. The wagon-yard door had been propped open, allowing the moist air of a mild Nebraska day, warm for early April, to circulate. Just now, the room was empty except for a clerk busy behind the counter. Channing went over and put down his bag. He was a sun-browned, clean-shaven man, his suit coat perhaps not quite wide enough for the broad shoulders, his pant legs worn outside cowhide boots. He caught the eye of the baldheaded clerk and asked for a ticket. "Dodge City."

"Straight through to Dodge, eh?" The man continued briskly as he wrote it up, "You're in luck. The coaches only go out twice a week right now, but it happens we got one leaving in an hour."

"So I was told. Business pretty good these days?"

"A little early in the season yet but fair—fair. This is kind of a pioneering operation. We already have stages running through this part of Nebraska, fanning out from the Union Pacific tracks. Now we're trying to make connections south of us, in Kansas—with the Kansas Pacific at Hays City and the Sante Fe at Dodge. If we can get a franchise to carry the mail, that will help. Sooner or later, the company hopes to blanket both states with

2

wagon and freight *and* stage service—every place the trains don't go."

"Sounds fine." Channing paid for his ticket, pocketed it, and cut the monologue short by asking, "Would you have paper and an envelope? I need to write a letter." The clerk produced the materials. "And where do I mail it when it's done?"

"Post office is up the street." He indicated a wooden box on the counter, a slot carved in its top. "Or you can drop it there."

Channing crossed the room to one of the benches, settled himself, and dug a pencil from his pocket. Using the grip he laid across his knees as a writing table, he addressed the envelope to Mrs. Maude Nolan, Laramie, Wyoming. The sheet of foolscap he headed "North Platte, Nebraska" and "April 10, 1878." He proceeded then to write in a firm, brisk hand:

Dear Maude:

This is just a note to let you know what's happening.

Up until yesterday, I was facing a blank wall and very near admitting this thing had me licked, but overnight matters have changed. The trail points to Dodge City, Kansas—according to the word I have now, Frank Killian seems to have surfaced there. I'm nearly certain this is no false lead, but at any rate it's the only lead I have, and I intend to follow up on it.

As long as there is any hope at all of squaring accounts for Tom Nolan, I'll never settle for less. That's a promise I make to Tom, to you, and to myself. So I'm off for Dodge, a three-day trip by stagecoach. I don't know what I'll find there, but I mean to be prepared for anything. I'll keep you posted.

With best regards,
Burl Channing

At nearly this same moment, in the crowded office of a mercantile establishment a few blocks from the stage station, a second letter was being written. Finished, Jared McAfee signed his name and then laid the steel-nibbed pen aside; he thoughtfully chewed at the inside of his lower lip while he considered what he had written. In contrast to the clutter of the desk from which he conducted his merchandising business and a sideline in land and cattle, he was a neat and well-dressed man, spare of frame, the full sideburns and wiry hair beginning to gray as he advanced into his forties.

Jared McAfee, satisfied with the letter, folded it and placed it in an envelope, which he laid, unsealed, in front of him; he removed gold-rimmed spectacles and dangled them between his fingers, considering. He got up, then opened the door of a second, smaller office. He said to the young woman working over a ledger, "Emily, would you step in a moment, please? I want to talk to you."

"Of course."

Emily Barker rose at once and joined him, primly taking the chair he indicated and waiting while he resumed his place. McAfee said, "I don't suppose you've had any more news. About your father?"

She soberly shook her head. "No, not since the telegram I showed you day before yesterday telling about the accident. My sister said it might be days yet before she'll know if it's serious enough that I should come home."

4

"But I take it you feel you ought to go, anyway."

Emily nodded. "Before I left, pa and I quarreled over my marrying Fred. I'd feel awfully bad to have that still hanging between us if—if something happens to him now."

"Yes, I understand. And that's the reason I've decided I want to help you."

Her head quickly lifted; her whole face seemed to light up. "Then you *are* going to lend me the fare? Oh, thank you, Mister McAfee! I hated asking, but—well, I simply don't have that much money, and I didn't know where I could raise it."

"I understand that, too," Jared McAfee said quickly, raising a hand. "You don't have to explain, not with your expenses during these months you've worked for me— your husband's sickness and all of that. If going back right now means so much to you, by all means I think you should go. Home is Springfield, Missouri—am I right?"

"Yes." She added, "And I promise to pay you back, every penny! I don't know how long it will take—but you must believe that!"

"Oh, I do. I do."

No one would be apt to doubt Emily Barker's sincerity. She was a young woman whose expressive face easily betrayed her emotions, and just now her brown eyes, behind dark lashes, actually shone with tears of gratitude. *A comely young woman*, Jared McAfee thought; he was as responsive as the next man to the trim figure in a white shirtwaist and skirt, a simple cameo pinned at her throat, the face with its wide brow and pleasant mass of dark curls. He was moved to answer gruffly, "I hope *you'll* believe that I'm going to hate to have you go. After all, I don't suppose there's any reason to expect we'll ever be seeing you here in Nebraska again.

I'll just have to try to find a replacement, and it may not be easy. You've been doing a fine job on those books."

"Thank you," she said. "It's something I learned from my father. He's a storekeeper, too, you know."

"I remember, you told me."

They were silent a moment. The room grew dark and then lighter again to the flow of cloud shadows, and a spatter of raindrops struck the windowpane. "Now, as for the money," McAfee said, "I have an assignment to offer you."

"An assignment?"

"I've written an important letter that needs delivering. This one." He held up the envelope. "It's addressed to a man named Frank Killian. Does the name mean anything to you?"

"No, I don't think so," she said. "Is it supposed to?"

"Probably not; he left North Platte sometime last summer, months before you came. It's been something of a mystery, and I've only just learned that the man has shown up again—in Dodge City, Kansas. It's most important that this should reach him without any delay. In fact, you could say it's a matter of life and death. No, I'm not just being melodramatic," he added, seeing the girl's expression. "I mean it quite literally."

"And you want *me* to deliver the letter?" She seemed puzzled. "To Dodge City?"

"It's not exactly on your way," he conceded. "In fact, it's a couple of hundred miles from here, almost due south. On the other hand, there's a stage leaving this morning, and once the letter has been turned over to Killian, you can catch a train east from there for Missouri. I wouldn't even suggest this if it wasn't so important. If you'll do it for me, in return I'm willing to put up the fare—all of it. No strings, no need to think about paying me back."

"Honest?" the girl exclaimed. "You mean it?"

"Absolutely. You'll have to decide soon, though. That stagecoach will be pulling out within the hour."

Still she hesitated. "If it's really so urgent, maybe you should send a telegram?"

"Naturally, I had the thought. But there's two reasons I decided against it: For one thing, I can't be absolutely sure of even a wire reaching him. Secondly, there's the message itself. . . ." As though on an impulse, he opened the envelope, took out the letter, and unfolded it, saying, "Perhaps you'll understand if I read you a couple of sentences—"

"It's not any of my business, Mister McAfee!"

"Still you'd have a right to wonder what you're getting yourself involved in. . . ." He fitted his spectacles in place, picked out the words he wanted from the body of the letter, and read aloud: "'I've met this Burl Channing briefly, and I know his reputation. I take it he's a lawman of sorts but primarily a killer—a hard and dangerous man. Right now it seems clear he means you for his next victim. The least I could do is try and get a warning to you in time.'" McAfee looked at Emily over the rims of his glasses. "Maybe that's enough to show why this whole thing is just too personal to put over the telegraph wires!"

The young woman across the desk from him had clearly been shocked by what she heard. "But surely—if you're dealing with a killer—there must be something the law could do!"

"This is the frontier, Emily," he replied solemnly as he returned the letter to its envelope. "I suppose Frank Killian *might* be able to get some help from the authorities

7

at Dodge if they happen to feel like it. There's nothing at all that *I* can do from this end."

"This Mister Killian must be a very close friend for you to be taking so much trouble."

"A friend?" McAfee repeated. He frowned as he removed the glasses, folded them, and tucked them into a pocket of his waistcoat. "That would be going a little too far—the man is, after all, a professional gambler! Let's just say I have reasons to feel a certain obligation. As for the trouble between him and this Burl Channing, it's their own affair. I simply think any man has the right to a warning when his life is in danger. Frank Killian deserves a chance to protect himself.

"Well, there's my proposition, Emily," he concluded. "I don't see how there could be any risk in it for you, but I'd be wrong to promise there isn't. If you'd rather not get mixed up in this—"

"Oh, no!" she said quickly. "I'll be glad to do it. But if I'm to catch the stage, I guess I'm going to have to hurry. And—oh, dear! There's the books. . . ."

"Don't give them a thought." He sealed the envelope containing the letter and passed it across the desk to her. "Keep good care of that," he warned. "Make sure nothing happens to it."

"Oh, of course! I won't let it out of my hands until I give it to Mister Killian."

"My best suggestion would be to ask directions to the Long Branch—I understand he's working there these days, running a faro game; someone should be able to tell you where to find him. Not that I like sending you to a saloon."

"That's perfectly all right," she assured him quickly. "I won't let it bother me. And if he's in Dodge City, I guarantee I'll find him!"

"Good enough." McAfee opened a drawer of the desk and took out a manila envelope containing a sheaf of greenbacks. He counted out several, saying, "Here's the salary you have coming, with enough to cover your fare and a little something extra to travel on." He got up and brought the money around the desk to her. As she took it, she seized his hand, smiling up at him warmly. "Thank you again, Mister McAfee. Thank you so much!"

"I thank *you*!" He patted her hand, holding it a little longer than was strictly necessary before he let it go. "Good-bye, Emily. I hope you have a good trip. If any further word should come for you, I'll send you a wire at Dodge."

When she hurried from the office, he stood for a long moment looking at the closed door. But now he was frowning with the manner of one who questions the wisdom of what he has done.

Within a block of the station, Emily knew she was cutting it fine. In the side yard, the coach was made up and ready, the four-horse team in the traces moving about restlessly amid the buzz of activity. Passengers mingled with the usual crowd of loafers here to watch the stage run pull out. The grizzled driver wrapped his reins about the brake pedal and climbed down to go into the station on some last-minute business. A few spears of rain shone, like golden streaks, in sunlight that filtered through the broken clouds.

Emily was already flustered and out of breath, suitcase in one hand and, in the other, a reticule that contained her money and the all-important letter with which she'd been entrusted. There had been no time in her hurry to pack properly or to do more than make a hasty change of clothes and throw together some spare garments and other necessities. Afterward, she had stood in her room at the boarding house looking about hopelessly at the rest of her belongings; but the landlady, a birdlike little woman, came in to tell her good-bye and to assure her she had no need to worry about her things—the few books, photographs of her family and of her husband, who had a few weeks ago died in that very room. The landlady would see they were collected and put in a box, to be sent on whenever she wrote for them.

"I just know we won't be seeing you here again," the woman had said, sniffling a little over the parting. "Not that I can blame you. This town has been a sad place for you—your poor husband struck down here in the midst of nowhere and you watching him die by inches, the doctor never even able to say what his trouble was!"

"The doctor did everything he could," Emily had insisted for perhaps the hundredth time. "You all did. You and Mister McAfee—everyone here has been just wonderful. But no, I'm not likely to be coming back to North Platte. Or going on to California, either. California was always Fred's idea. I'd have no business out there now—alone."

"A person belongs just one place," the woman said firmly. "I'm glad you're going home. You need your family. And don't fret too much about your father's accident. I'm sure he's going to be all right."

"I do hope so. Poor pa! We love each other dearly, but we just can't seem to get along. My sister says it's because we're too much alike—both of us too stubborn for our own good!"

After the unhappiness of the last four months, Emily told herself as she set down her heavy bag before the station doorway, she could have few regrets at leaving this place—this raw division point on the Union Pacific in the flatlands of Nebraska. A distant wailing of a train whistle came to her from somewhere along the Platte valley; the lonely sound reminded her sharply of the day when a hopeful journey west was suddenly disrupted, Fred being taken off the train with a sudden fever no one had been able to diagnose. Some kind of infection, the doctor said. Ten nightmare weeks she had fought to save him. And now she was going, leaving him behind forever in the local cemetery—the husband she had known for such a little while that, to the end, he had never really been more than a pleasant stranger who had turned cranky and demanding in the last, wearing illness.

What strange, sad ways fate had with us sometimes. . . .

A man's voice said, "Ma'am, if you figure to make this stage, you haven't got much time. We're just about to roll."

She looked up, a little startled, into an unsmiling, sun-browned face beneath a flat-brimmed, low-crowned hat—a face, she thought, that appeared strong rather than handsome. Something in the tall man's regard as he held the door he had opened for her made her feel suddenly flushed and warm and disheveled. She explained lamely, "I had to catch my breath—I've been practically running! Is that the southbound coach?"

"Straight through to Dodge City. You have your ticket?"

"No. I suppose I'd better hurry and buy it."

"Yes, ma'am." He pointed to the heavy bag. "Can I help you with that?"

"Well—" She hesitated, suddenly wary, telling herself that a woman alone could never be certain she would not be victimized and taken advantage of. She had a vision of this stranger making off with her bag; perhaps he

11

was secretly eying her reticule, wondering how much money she might be carrying. But she looked again at the thoughtfully solemn face, and something about it gave her confidence in him. "That's kind of you. Thank you very much."

At the desk, he showed no interest at all in the money she took out to pay for her ticket; he seemed more concerned with the final departure preparations going on in the yard. When she was ready, he took her bag again and walked with her to the side door where he said, "I'll have this put in the luggage boot. You'd better get right on if you want a good seat."

"Are you going through to Dodge City?" Emily asked out of curiosity, and he nodded as he gave her a hand into the coach.

She found a place by a window. Another woman, with the look of a settler's wife, was already aboard, and now a portly man in a plug hat and side whiskers came puffing up the high iron step and wedged himself between them. When the man who had disposed of Emily's bag came to join the company, the only place left for him was on the forward seat, just behind the driver's box, where he would have to ride facing backwards. He laid a cool, assessing glance on his fellow passengers, let his dark eyes linger for a moment on Emily's face, and then turned to the window beside him.

Looking at him in profile as he peered out into the thin rain, Emily was struck again by something brooding and withdrawn, something that intrigued and attracted her in the sun-darkened cheeks and the definite line of his jaw.

Everything seemed ready at last. The horses were stomping in the traces. Charlie, the driver—a stringbean figure, poncho clad, with straggling whiskers and a tremendous wad of tobacco seemingly lodged permanently in one cheek—completed a final meticulous check on the harnessing of his team. He swung easily up the hub of the big front wheel to his place. An excited dog started barking. Someone in the yard crew yelled an obscene joke, and the driver answered in kind, making the other woman passenger gasp with affronted modesty. Emily Barker, for her part, had to turn her head away and hide a smile.

The brake was booted off; a yell sent the team surging into their collars. And at that moment a shout came from the station doorway: "Hey, Charlie—hold it! You got another fare to Dodge City!"

Charlie swore luridly and tromped his brake, and the coach rocked violently as the split reins curbed the horses to a stand. The door was wrenched open, and a man hurriedly ducked inside to drop into an unoccupied corner of the forward seat. Even as he pulled the door shut behind him, Charlie could be heard, exclaiming belligerently, "That had better be *it*. Because—by God, I'm rolling!" And to the slap of reins the coach rocked forward, the passengers grabbing for the tug straps. The horses were already approaching a gallop as they broke out of the station yard and turned along the puddled street, making for the open Nebraska prairie.

The newcomer showed no signs of fluster. Not even breathing hard, he nodded to the others and said calmly enough, "My apologies." Burl Channing turned from the window for a look at the man on the seat beside him, and it was as though something might have tripped a warning bell. His appearance—the slender figure, the shape of the hands that held a leather bag on his knees, the somehow predatory features and the hooded eyes—somehow spelled danger. Channing, who had a gun and holster and shell belt packed in a valise stowed under his seat, would be willing to bet this latest addition to the company had a weapon even closer at hand than that—perhaps in the bag he held on his lap, perhaps hidden somewhere in his clothing. This man had the look of a professional gunman.

If so, he might prove to be an asset on the stage journey across the empty, lawless miles of the plains, with Dodge City a long three days ahead of them.

Chapter 2

Once across the South Platte River, the road ran straight, twin ruts cut into prairie sod by the stages and freight wagons that chiefly used it. Burl Channing, who had been through this country before, knew the land would lie almost unbroken until they got into the system of shallow, eastward-flowing rivers—the Republican, the Solomon, the Saline, and the Smoky Hill—that braided the map of western Nebraska and Kansas like the ends of frayed ropes.

Past the open windows flowed a changeless grassland, nearly treeless except for cottonwoods and willows along the creek beds. With two days and nights of travel ahead, the coach and teams had quickly settled into a rhythm that alternated between a walk and a shuffling, mile-consuming trot. Above the steady sound of wheels and iron-shod hoofs, a stream of profanity came back from the horse-hating driver on the box. Venting his emotions on his animals seemed to have no effect at all in their unvarying, efficient work in the harness.

" Well! " The portly traveler with the whiskers slapped both chubby palms on his knees and peered about him at the women crowded on either side and the men facing him on the opposite seat. "Here we all are—fellow passengers. Looks like we'll be seeing quite a lot of each other, if you follow me." He accompanied that with a wink at the farm woman and got nothing more than a cool stare in return.

Undaunted, he continued, "Situation like this, I always say the proper thing is for everyone to break the ice and get acquainted. Murtaugh's the name—John Murtaugh; Jack to all my friends. I'm in gents' and ladies' furnishings. Cover a two-state area and doing real well, thank you! But don't worry, folks! I got no use for a pest; I'm not going to insist on showing you my catalogues— my business is strictly wholesale. Somebody else's turn now," he finished, and put a bright and expectant eye on the rest of the party. "Who'll be next? You, sir?" He nodded to the one Burl Channing had pegged for a gunman. "What name are we to know you by?"

This time, even his thick hide could not turn aside the edge of the piercing stare he received. Then the man he'd addressed simply turned and looked out the window, leaving Jack Murtaugh to grow slowly red of face. Channing, observing this, could almost feel sorry for the salesman, but it was really his own fault. By being too assertive, he had put everyone off and spoiled his chances of thawing the chilly reserve among the people in the coach. All the spirit seemed to run out of him, rather like the collapse of a pricked balloon. His face fell, and his shoulders slumped, and he sank back into his place; from then on, everyone carefully avoided looking at him.

So they rode in total silence to the sway of the coach on its thoroughbraces, alternating light and shadow flowing across the land as the spring sun worked its way through a broken cloud field overhead. A squall of rain blew in through the open windows, causing a quick flurry of canvas curtains being unrolled and buttoned down. Channing watched the girl work with hers; he would have liked to help, but she was on the opposite side of the coach from him. She managed well enough, however. Later, she caught him looking at her and gave him a quick smile. It was unexpected, and it warmed him with pleasure.

But then his purpose in Dodge City—a matter that was never far from his thoughts—surfaced again and pushed other things aside in bleak speculation.

It was a little later that Jack Murtaugh committed his second social error: He came up out of a brooding silence to take a leather case from his inside coat pocket, remove the lid, and extract a fat, black cigar. He examined it carefully and with approval, licked a frayed tab of tobacco, and molded it into place with his fingers. He was just placing the end between his teeth to bite it off when Channing said shortly, "I don't think you better do that."

The drummer stared at him and then at the cigar. "You have some objection, mister?"

"The ladies might. Least you can do is ask."

It seemed to be something he had never thought about. "Well, now," he said. "How about it? Anybody here mind a little good tobacco smoke? These ain't any cheap stogies, you understand. They're the best—straight from Havana. Cost me a nickel apiece!"

It was the homesteader's woman, seated at his right, who told him stiffly, "If you *don't* mind . . ."

"Why of course! All you need to do is mention it, lady. Anyone'll tell you Jack Murtaugh is an obliging fellow."

The drummer made an airy gesture, but he looked somewhat disgruntled as he started to put his smoke away. But now Burl Channing's seat companion twisted about to thrust his head through the open window and call forward to the driver: "Pull up a second."

"Why the hell should I?" Charlie Pitts wanted to know.

"There's a passenger wants to come up on the box and have a smoke."

That brought an outburst of the driver's lurid language. "You think I ain't got a schedule to meet, that I can be stopping every five minutes!" But he hauled in his team, and the lean man unhooked the door and let it swing open.

"There you are," he told Jack Murtaugh briefly. If the drummer felt he'd been insulted by this ejection, he covered it with a shrug. He scrambled out awkwardly, tipped his hat to the women as he slammed the door, and moments later had managed to hoist himself up the big front wheel to the place beside the driver; with a shout, Charlie Pitts got his horses into motion again.

Emily Barker gave a smile to the pair on the other seat. "Thank you," she said. "Thank you both! I'm sure Mister Murtaugh is well-meaning, but his manners *are* a little crude."

The slim one, the one who had nearly missed catching the stage back at North Platte, shrugged and said, "The fellow is an ass!"

Nevertheless, the ice had been broken, and the atmosphere in the coach improved perceptibly. "He was probably right, though," Emily said. "We all really ought to introduce ourselves since we have to travel together. My name's Emily Barker."

Channing indicated the gold band on her hand. "That's *Mrs.* Barker?"

Her eyes dropped to the ring, and her smile faded. "Yes, but—my husband died, quite recently."

"Oh!" It left him with nothing to say except an awkward "Sorry!" that sounded rough and curt in his own ear. He added, "I'm Burl Channing."

What happened next was startling. To Channing's

18

amazement, she seemed to stiffen. Her head slowly lifted, and her eyes sought his; her face had gone suddenly slack, almost as though with horror. Returning her look, completely puzzled, he only half heard the other woman say that her name was Anna Schulte and that she was returning to her homestead on the Smoky Hill after visiting relatives near Ogallala. And the man on the seat beside him added, "That leaves me, I guess. I answer to Wes Lowe. . . ."

Burl Channing was still watching the young woman, trying to fathom the sudden change in her. Groping for words—not being a man for whom any kind of small talk came easily, especially with a woman—he managed to get out, "You been to Dodge City before, Mrs. Barker?"

She merely regarded him, not answering; then, deliberately, she turned her head and gave her attention to the drab scenery moving past her window. Channing was left at a loss, knowing only that for some reason any trace of her earlier warmth and friendliness was gone. All at once, he thought it wouldn't be too hard to understand how poor Jack Murtaugh must have felt, being frozen out.

It was sometime later that Channing realized, with a start, he remembered where it was he had heard the name Wes Lowe before.

They pulled into a station presently for a change of horses and a meal. Channing got out and waited by the coach to help the women take the long step to the ground. Emily Barker quickly withdrew her hand from his, and when he said, "It feels good to get out and move around a little," he got only the briefest of glances before she hurried on into the station, as though she could not get away from him fast enough.

This time there was no mistaking the snub, and Channing found himself growing angry. "All right, ma'am," he muttered to himself. "I won't bother you again!" And then he caught an amused, sidelong glance from Wes Lowe as the man went by. He wondered if he had said the words aloud and felt his face flush at the thought that he probably had.

The stop was actually a homestead layout, doubling as a station for a fee from the stage company. House and barn were both constructed from the tough prairie sod. They were dirt floored; only the partitions, door, and window framings were made of crudely sawed cottonwood boards. Platters of steak and fried potatoes and thick-sliced bread, jars of wild plum jam and pickles, and a couple of dried-apple pies had already been set out on the trestle table by the homesteader's wife and daughter; coffee thick as tar was being poured out of iron pots black from the fireplace coals.

Having washed up at the bench beside the door, Burl Channing took a seat at the opposite end of the table from where the female passengers were eating together. The food was about what could be expected, and he filled his plate and worked at it stolidly, knowing that under the constant pressure to keep to the schedule, there was never enough time for meals. Already, through the open doorway, he could watch the horses being taken off the pole, to be replaced by new teams from the corral.

Finished, he went outside and found Wes Lowe walking about, taking the chance to stretch his legs. The clouds were scattering, and a warm sun was drawing tendrils of steam from the flat, wet prairie. "Drying out," Channing observed, and the other man nodded. They watched Charlie Pitts supervising carefully the hitching of the restless new teams. Jack Murtaugh came from the outhouse and entered the station, giving no more than a chill glance at his fellow passengers.

Presently, Channing said, "I think I know you—or know of you. You're the same Wes Lowe that killed the Olin brothers in Tascosa last year: Bob and Phin. I think there was another one in the fight, too. Some shirttail kin of the Olins."

The other man's face had gone perfectly expressionless. "Dick Reeder," he supplied. "A cousin of sorts. But he wasn't much better than a half-wit—he didn't affect the odds, to speak of."

"Still I heard it was a fight. That whole outfit was known to be horse thieves, with Bob supposedly the worst. I never actually met up with him, but I ran into some of the others over in the nations."

"I'm not surprised." And then the lean face, with its sardonic expression, turned to regard Channing directly. "Less surprised," Wes Lowe added dryly, "than I am to be running into *you* here in Nebraska! You're a little out of your territory, aren't you? I could ask what one of Ike Parker's marshals is doing this far north of Fort Smith."

So it seemed, in the way of their kind on the frontier, these two had recognized each other from their names and reputations alone—one of them a gunman, the other an officer of the court appointed by Judge Isaac Parker, who, after three years on the bench for the Western District of Arkansas, with jurisdiction over the Indian territory west of Fort Smith, was already beginning to be known as a "hanging" judge.

Standing there in the sun, before that sod hovel of a stage station, they sized one another up—not with hostility or enmity, merely a kind of professional curiosity. And Burl Channing, in answer to the other's question, said bluntly, "I'm not wearing my badge on this trip; I'm on leave of absence to take care of a personal matter that has nothing to do with Judge Parker or the law."

If Wes Lowe had further questions just then, he kept them to himself, perhaps because he suspected he had learned as much as this sun-browned, black-eyed man was of a mind to tell him. Also, at that moment, Charlie Pitts came striding toward the station, singing out in his carrying voice, "All right, you pilgrims! Now let's get loaded up. We ain't keeping a schedule this way!"

And so the journey was resumed—a journey that by now had already settled into a numbing monotony. The horses slogged on at a gait that in an hour covered perhaps five miles of flat and almost featureless land, with stops only to change teams at identical homestead soddies or at some drab little prairie town containing a barn and a store and a saloon. Even the heavy thoroughbraces could not absorb all the jolting of iron-tired wheels in narrow and unpaved tracks. A person clung to the tug strap by his seat and took the jolts and the swaying, looking out at the sameness of the scenery.

There was not much talking. Once Emily Barker asked in a tired voice, "Do I understand we keep going all night? We don't stop at all?"

Burl Channing answered her. "I'm afraid that's right. This stage line is only a feeder to connect the railroads. Tomorrow we'll reach Hays City on the Kansas Pacific, and the next evening we'll be at Dodge; but there's no other layovers. Tonight we have to make do the best we can."

That got him no more than an unfriendly stare, but for whatever reason it was by now all he had come to expect. Later, when he happened to look in her direction, he twice caught her watching him with a speculative frown; she turned away as soon as their eyes met. But it left him more puzzled than ever.

Presently, the two women fell to talking, and he heard her telling Mrs. Schulte something about herself—about her husband's death in North Platte, about a recent accident in which her father had been seriously injured by the failing of the brake on a wagon he had been unloading at his store in a town in southern Missouri. Because of this, she was on her way home, with some business that must be tended to in Dodge City on the way. It struck Burl Channing as a peculiarly roundabout course, but by this time he knew better than to ask her any questions—or even speak to her.

The afternoon drew out; the sun sank in a smear of yellow against the flat horizon. With dusk, a chill breeze came off the prairie, and they rolled down and fastened the leather curtains; later, at a supper stop, Jack Murtaugh approached Channing to say gruffly, "It's going to start getting kind of crisp up there on that box. I'm moving back inside."

"I'll trade with you," Channing suggested, "if you'll take my place and let the women have that other seat between them. Perhaps they can make themselves comfortable and manage to get some sleep."

"That's all right, I guess."

So when they pulled out again, Channing was on the box beside the driver. They had picked up a new one at this stop, Charlie Pitts being replaced by a man who did his work silently and without any of Pitts's steady stream of profanity. Channing felt no inclination to talk. He braced himself against the sway of his high seat, turned up his coat collar, and shoved his hands into his pockets. The black night engulfed them—a dome of brilliant stars overhead, the lanterns of the coach lighted now and throwing a fitful gleam over the undulating ground close beside the coach. The horses worked steadily, smoothly, and surefootedly as the night grew deeper.

Sometime before daybreak, they crossed an invisible line into Kansas. The coach passengers roused themselves stiffly to face a second long day of travel.

When the lights of Hays City showed up on the flat plain, promising a night's rest before the final haul to their destination at Dodge, Emily Barker felt she was nearer to exhaustion than at any other time since Fred's last illness. After the intermittent rain squalls of the previous day, it had been a day of blazing sunlight, of gritty dust, and of pummeling wind that had seemed enough at times to knock the coach off its wheels. There had been the dry smell of the dust that got into her hair and her clothing, the constant popping of gusty wind in the leather curtain close beside her face—this after a night in which she had not really been able to sleep but only to doze fitfully. Her spirits rose as she remembered they would be getting out of the coach here for a night in a real bed.

They pulled up in front of a two-story box of a hotel, and while they stood about waiting for their luggage to be taken from the boot, Emily had a look along the wide street. Dusk was nearly complete, only a last gleam of yellow showing along the horizon; the town itself, with Fort Hays no more than a couple of miles away, already showed plenty of life, with stores and saloons lighted and going full blast and blue-clad troopers cruising the sidewalks.

Anna Schulte, with whom she had become quite friendly during two days on the stage, came to Emily to say good-bye—her son, a gangling youngster on the seat

24

of a farm wagon, had been waiting to pick her up and take her the half-dozen miles to their homestead. Emily was sorry to see her go; it left her feeling very much alone to watch Anna climb to the wagon seat and go off into the gathering night. This was the only other woman she knew in this whole state of Kansas. So it was in a measure reassuring when, having collected her bag from the stage driver, she entered the hotel and found a woman in charge.

She was given the key to a room on the second floor; she asked, "Would it be possible to have some hot water sent up? I won't feel human until I've had a chance to clean up a little."

"Why sure, honey," the proprietress told her. "But supper's just about on the table. If you're late, you'll miss out."

Emily thanked her and went up the stairs, a hand on the rail to steady her—her knees were all but shaking with fatigue. It felt strange to have something solid under her feet again. Her small room held only the bare essentials: a rickety bed, a dresser, and a single straight chair. But she would have been glad enough to drop full length on the sagging bed just as she was. Instead, she forced the window open, using a piece of stick to prop it, and stood a moment looking into the lamp-lit street, listening to the sounds of the early night.

There was a knock at the door, and a girl from the kitchen came in with a steaming bucket of water. Emily would have liked a complete bath and a change of clothing. Tomorrow night, perhaps, at Dodge? She filled the chipped porcelain basin and washed up as best she could. She shook the dust from her skirt and blouse and put them back on, then did something with her hair. By that time, she realized how starved she was, and she lost no more time in heading downstairs for the dining room where she could hear the sound of voices, the clink of china and silverware.

Part way down, she halted suddenly, seeing Burl Channing emerge through the doorway of the dining room.

He paused and stood with his head down and hands thrust into trouser pockets as though immersed in thought. Emily drew back a little into the shadows, not liking to spy but reluctant to confront him alone there in the dingy hotel lobby. Looking down at the man, unobserved, she was struck again by a strange confusion in her feelings—remembering how favorably he had impressed her in their moment of meeting in the Nebraska stage office, and then the sudden shock at hearing his name and recognizing it as the one in the letter she carried in her reticule. He was the reason she was making this hurried trip to Dodge City. A killer, Jared McAfee had labeled him, and she knew her employer to be a man who made sure of his facts. The shock and disappointment were made worse by knowing that once she reached Dodge, pressure would be on her to get to Frank Killian first with word that a man who meant to kill him had arrived on the same stagecoach as she.

A second man came from the dining room; this was the man who called himself Wes Lowe. Of the two, she would have been somehow much more apt to think of him as the dangerous one—unlike Channing, there had been something about him that put her on her guard at once. An unlikely pair, Lowe and Channing had apparently been strangers, but now they appeared to have struck up a friendship. Two of a kind, perhaps?

It seemed that Channing had been waiting for the other man; they fell into step and crossed the lobby, talking, going out on to the porch of the hotel to pause there a moment, looking at the night. Then she saw them start out together, like good friends with a common aim of having a look at this Hays City.

It was only when she was sure they were gone that Emily came the rest of the way down the stairs to enter the dining room.

Chapter 3

The stage passengers weren't given too much time to enjoy their hard beds and musty blankets. The new driver wanted an early start, and it was still dark when they assembled again, chilled and only half awake, to wait with their baggage on the porch for the stage to be brought around. There was to be one new passenger for Dodge City—a man named Hotchkiss who said he was a lawyer with some business at the Ford County courthouse. The driver for this last day turned out to be a red-whiskered and genial giant of a fellow named Tug Wheeler, whose huge fists engulfed the double reins and who seemed to enjoy himself and his job.

On the whole, Burl Channing thought he would have a pleasanter time of it on the box chatting with this friendly man than enduring the chill animosity of Emily Barker in the coach; and Wheeler seemed to welcome Channing's company. He was seated up there as the coach pulled out of Hays City, with the cool April morning lying upon the Kansas prairie.

Tug Wheeler was a veteran. He told Channing he had driven for Ben Holladay in the last great days of the Overland; that was just before the laying of the Union Pacific's rails from the Missouri River to the ocean put an end to an era of transcontinental staging. Wheeler was philosophical about finding himself driving for a feeder line, hauling passengers the few miles between one railroad and another; one thing you could count on things doing, he said, was changing. He knew how to handle his horses; he kept them into their collars, yet without wearing them down, he managed to put a lot of miles under the wheels of his stage as the hours dragged by. "If you're going somewhere," he commented, "you might as well get gone!"

"How are things in Dodge?" Channing asked him.

"Lively for this early in the season. The big herds from Texas will be coming in any time now, and that will really pull the stopper out. You familiar with Dodge City?"

"Been there a couple of times. The last was in seventy-five, and it was pretty wild then. Has the political situation changed any since?"

"Well, there was a law-and-order faction took over for a while, but now they're out, and the old Dodge City gang is back in control. That's Bob Wright and 'Dog' Kelley and the other big-money men who want a wide-open town; this bunch wants to keep the Texans happy and spending cash. Kelley's the mayor, and he's put Ed Masterson in as town marshal. You know Ed?"

"Never met him. I know his brother Bat."

"Ed Masterson's a good man but maybe too likable and easygoing. Not quite mean enough, I'd have thought, for a tough job. Bat, on the other hand, he's been sheriff of Ford County since the first of the year, and he's riding high since he brought in the gang that tried to knock off the Sante Fe train over to Kinsley. People have got a lot of respect for Bat Masterson even if they like Ed better."

29

Later, in the course of one of their talks, Channing took the chance of asking, "I wonder if you'd happen to know anything about a man named Frank Killian?"

"The name don't register."

"He might not have been around more than a few months. I understand he's running a faro bank in one of the saloons—the Long Branch, or so I was told."

"Oh." The driver's red-whiskered, sun-whipped face took on a sour look. "Well, I don't have nothing to do with that breed! Them professionals—for my money, every one of 'em is either a crook or at least halfway crazy. I never knowed anybody like a gambler for superstition. If they figure their luck is in, then they're ten feet tall; but once it sets against 'em, they crumble to nothing. I say a man makes his own luck. I got no use at all for one that tries to lay the blame on the way a bunch of dumb cards happen to be running!"

"I couldn't argue with that."

They crossed the Smoky Hill, Walnut Creek, the Pawnee—another day of sun and buffeting wind and dust that got into eyes and teeth and made the horses toss their heads resentfully; another day of rest stops and stops for fresh horses and for the noon meal at a homestead soddy. It was tedious but otherwise without any real incident until late afternoon. Then, taking the shallow drop into a dry creek bed, the coach hit a spot where recent rains had softened and broken down the packed sand.

Tug Wheeler had pulled in his horses and slammed one foot on the brake before starting down, but the heavy coach began to slew sideways, and Channing caught at the grabiron, half expecting the entire rig to go over with its teams in a thrashing, fatal tangle. But Wheeler was a better hand than that. Without losing his calm, he threw his weight against the leathers; the horses straightened

30

out, and they brought up at the foot of the bank in a cascading of silt, but with no damage done.

The big man's only comment was a laconic "Bad spot there."

There were startled cries from inside the coach—Channing recognized Jack Murtaugh's voice and the lawyer's, but there was no sound at all from the woman or from Wes Lowe. That didn't really surprise him. Unlike as they were, it had seemed to him that Emily Barker and the gunman had that much at least in common: They were both levelheaded, both able to keep cool in a moment of danger.

He could imagine the Barker woman, white of face and clinging to her seat during that perilous moment when it must have seemed as though the lumbering vehicle was about to go over. Still, she rode it out in silence. Channing was thinking mainly of her as he called down reassuringly, "It's all right. Everything's fine— nothing to worry about."

Wheeler concentrated on his horses, calming them and giving them a moment to sort themselves out. He was occupied with this when a pair of riders eased out of the shadow of some scrub timber and reined over toward the motionless stage.

To Channing, it looked as though they could have been waiting for something like this. He drew the driver's attention to them; Wheeler lifted his big head and gave them a suspicious look as they pulled up. "Well?"

They could have been cowboys, or they could have been tramps. Their horses were scrubby, and so likewise were men, clothing, and gear. One, a towheaded fellow whose cheeks appeared to be peeling from chronic sunburn, tilted his head to squint from under the brim of a battered hat and inquire, "This the road to Dodge?"

31

"I imagine you know since you're on it," Tug Wheeler said curtly. "Where the hell did you two show up from so sudden. Just what do you want?"

"Well, see," the second man told him, "it's a stickup." And with a single movement, they each brought a gun sliding out of holster.

"A stickup!" Tug Wheeler echoed in a roar. He and Channing looked into the muzzles of .45s pointing at their faces.

Neither man on the box was armed. Channing's pistol was in his bag inside the coach. There was a carbine in the boot, out of reach. He didn't make any attempt to get it now, with two revolvers covering him. Instead, he looked back at the pair and said with heavy scorn, "You must be strangers for sure! This is a poverty outfit you're looking at. There's nothing aboard worth stealing. Not even a mail sack—the line has got no franchise."

"That's all right," the one with the sunburn assured him. "You got what we want, all right. Four of 'em."

Tug Wheeler saw the direction of the robber's look. The driver seemed to swell in size, and his face got red with anger. "You ain't taking these horses!"

The second bandit, a thin fellow with a scruff of unshaven black whiskers and a habitual sneer, suggested, "Would you like to stick around and see? There's a good market in these parts just now for anything that wears hoofs and a tail." He looked at his companion. "Dave, I'll keep an eye on things here. You fetch the rest of them outside."

Nodding, the towhead kneed his animal around so that he could cover the door of the coach. "Everybody out!" he ordered. "Don't try any tricks or I'll have to shoot you."

The door swung open. First to emerge was Jack

32

Murtaugh; the drummer had his hands high, and he wore a look of fright. "Careful with that gun, damn it!" he exclaimed as he reached for the ground with a polished, high-button shoe. "I ain't going to try anything. I ain't armed!"

"Then you got nothing to worry about, have you?" It struck Channing, alertly watching, that the sunburned rider was nervous, tensed up for this. Highway robbery was probably a new undertaking for him, yet being green and scared would not make him or the gun in his hand any less of a danger.

The lawyer was next to descend and then Emily Barker. She had her reticule clutched tightly. As she saw the bandit eying it, she exclaimed in a small voice, "This is every cent I own. Please don't take it!" He made no move to, and now Wes Lowe stepped down to join the others.

Channing had been curious to see Lowe's reaction to a holdup, but he showed no sign at all of resisting. He merely lined up beside the now-empty coach, expressionless, his hands obediently raised. "Is that all of them?" Dave's partner wanted to know, and at the affirmative nod he said gruffly, "Then let's get on with it!"

"I have no intention," Wes Lowe announced, "of being killed over a gold watch. You might as well take this right now." He reached toward a waistcoat pocket as though to fetch it out, but when he completed the movement, what he had in his hand was not a timepiece but a .38 caliber revolver from the shoulder holster Burl Channing suspected was hidden under his coat. The draw was done so casually that the towheaded bandit was caught staring.

He was still staring when Wes Lowe shot him.

The report cracked flatly. The bullet could have done no more than nick the man in the arm, but it jarred a yell of pain from him and sent his revolver spinning out of his hand. Lowe was already turning to look for the second horseman, who seemed to be reacting more quickly than his friend had; even as Lowe was swiveling on one foot, the man on horseback brought his gun over and fired at him.

It was too hurried, and it missed. A neat round hole stamped itself in the paneling of the coach near Lowe's elbow. Jack Murtaugh gave a yelp of fear and dived headlong to the loose sand of the creek bottom; the lawyer, Hotchkiss, with better self-control, dropped to one knee so as to make a smaller target. But Channing saw that Emily Barker had frozen motionless, as though too surprised to move at all—she stood there in full range of another wild bullet from the stage robber. Wes Lowe, for his part, did not waste a move. He fired into the balloon of smoke from the bandit's gun, the two reports mingling.

The man was wiped out of the saddle, tumbling from sight. All the horses of the stage teams were pitching and squealing with terror, but Tug Wheeler's big boot, set firmly on the brake, helped hold them in place. Belatedly, then, Burl Channing thought of the carbine in the boot of the stage. He scrambled for it and brought it up, but there was nothing to use it on.

The dead bandit had caught his foot in the stirrup, and his weight held the frightened mount in place so that it only moved in a tight circle, the man's head and shoulders dragging loosely. Yonder, his towheaded companion had recovered from the shock of having his gun shot out of his hand. Seeing everything gone to hell, he had jerked his horse around and with boots flailing was sending it away at a run up the creek bed. Wes Lowe moved out a few paces and took deliberate aim, but just as he fired, the horse took a sidestep. Next moment, animal and rider were into the trees.

Burl Channing lowered the carbine without firing it, then came down off the box. By the time Tug Wheeler had his frenzied teams quieted and clambered down to join the others, Channing had caught the riderless horse and was holding it steady while Wes Lowe freed the dead man's foot from the stirrup. They stood and looked at him—his whiskered face slack, his chest smeared with blood.

To someone's query, the stage driver denied recognizing the holdup man, saying, "This country's full of petty crooks—that's why they've made Bat Masterson sheriff. We got this horse," he added, slapping its rump with a broad palm. "Any volunteers to mount up and go after the other one?"

Nobody was interested. Channing said, "We've all got business of our own. Besides, he has too good a lead. It'll be getting dark in an hour or so."

Wheeler said, "All right, we'll just load this one on his saddle and put him on a tow line. Take him in for Bat."

Jack Murtaugh had recovered from the moment of panic that had sent him hugging the ground while the guns were firing. Wiping his plug hat clean with a handkerchief, he told Wes Lowe, "At least you got one out of two. That wasn't bad."

That got him a cold look from the gunman, who had by now replaced the spent bullets and returned his gun to its place under his coat. "One out of two? You're mistaken, mister. The first one, I only meant to disarm. This second man could have killed somebody, shooting wild; he didn't give me any choice."

The drummer, taken aback by the chill correction, nodded and quickly said, "I get your point. That was *very* good shooting, friend—I'll be the first to say it!"

35

As Wheeler and the lawyer turned to the grisly task of lifting the dead man across his saddle, Burl Channing went to where Emily stood. "Are you all right?"

She looked pale and shaken, but at his question she managed a nod and told him briefly, "I'm quite all right. Thank you."

"I guess we're about ready to go on," Channing said. "We might as well load up." When she turned to mount the high iron step into the coach, he took her elbow and thought he could feel her still trembling.

When they came down off the low bluff rimming the wide Arkansas valley on the north, a swollen sun lay against the horizon; it burnished the river to gold, made molten streaks of the Santa Fe's twin rails that lay this side of it, and gave a kind of beauty to the sprawl of low buildings that was Dodge City. The sight stirred Emily Barker out of the weary lethargy from three days of travel, tightening the screws of nervous tension all over again as she realized the hour for completing her mission here was now almost at hand.

The horses seemed to pick up spirit with the knowledge that their work was nearly over. It didn't take the whip to increase their speed and bring the coach barreling in that last mile. The buildings seemed to swell and grow as the town took on shape. The spire of a church on one of the high points of the nearly flat terrain gleamed with the setting sun and then faded as the light left it. The sun had just dipped out of sight when they rolled into the town itself.

Apparently, the stage line had no station here; instead, the coach pulled up at the wooden railroad depot beside the Santa Fe tracks that split the heart of Dodge City. Tug Wheeler tromped the brake lever, bringing his teams to a snorting halt and making the old coach rock for a last time on its thorough braces. "Dodge City, folks," he announced in a carrying voice. "End of the line. You'll find accommodations at the Dodge House, across Front Street on your right."

Emily stepped down, uncertain of her next move. She thought the Dodge House, a two-story, clapboard-and-whitewash structure, with a vacant lot on one side of it and a billiard hall on the other, didn't look too promising. Westward from the hotel, false-fronted business houses stood packed in a solid row with the town's residential section behind them. Across the tracks from Front Street lay a weed-grown expanse of ground four blocks long that Emily understood was called "the Plaza."

There on the south side of town were the saloons, dance halls, and red-light district Anna Schulte had told her about in whispered confidences during the long stage journey. This part of town gave Dodge City its reputation as the wickedest town on the frontier. Emily thought it all seemed peaceable enough in this first hour after sunset, but she supposed there could be quite a different story once night fell.

Just now the arrival of the stage had brought a crowd gathering, and from the excited talk and movement that eddied about her, Emily knew it was the led horse and its limp burden that attracted these Front Street men who had the frontier's sure instinct for violence. She hesitated, carefully not looking at the dead man and thinking of her bag stowed under the canvas flap of the rear boot. It was then that she heard Burl Channing's voice beside her. "Mrs. Barker?"

She looked up. With the cool civility of one who guards against a rebuff, he said, "It don't look like much, but the Dodge House is about as good as the town has to

37

offer. If you want to go sign in, I'll be glad to fetch your bag for you."

Studying his dark and expressionless face, Emily decided that he was really trying to be helpful, and she supposed she should be grateful. But the one thing she had to do right away was to get away from here—away from him—without arousing suspicion. She made herself nod and say, "Thank you. I'd appreciate that."

"It may take me a minute," he said, "with all this crowd. You go on in the lobby, and I'll bring it to you there."

She nodded again, and he turned to work his way into the increasingly noisy knot of bystanders clustering around the coach. At once, Emily started across the wheel-rutted street toward the hotel, stepping up to the uneven wooden sidewalk. But she didn't mount the steps to the porch. She turned instead along the walk, determined to put distance behind her while Channing was preoccupied.

The trouble was that she had no idea how to find the place she was looking for. The need for haste gave her the courage to ask directions from a man loitering in front of J. Mueller's boot shop, where he was watching in idle curiosity the people swirling about the stagecoach.

He looked her over, a deliberate inspection that made the breath catch in her throat and the heat mount into her cheeks. He clearly had his opinion of a woman who would want to know the way to a saloon. But he hitched himself from leaning against the shop front. "You want the Long Branch?" He pointed west along the street. "The end of the next block. You see a big, two-story building on the corner of Bridge Street?"

"I—guess so."

"Well, that ain't it—that's Bob Wright's store. The Long Branch is two doors this side."

"Thank you," she said, and went on her way before he might feel encouraged to add something more personal.

Ignoring curious stares, she hurried past one shabby-looking business enterprise after another, hardly noticing the signs they carried—a land office, the Dodge Opera House, the Alamo Saloon, the City Drug Store, Beatty and Kelley's Alhambra Saloon, the Delmonico Restaurant, a tonsorial parlor and a gun store, a dry goods establishment. . . . Occasionally, she paused for an anxious look back, afraid to see Channing coming behind her and making for the same destination. Though she failed to see him, her knees shook, and the breath seemed locked in her chest.

But now at last she was nearing the end of the second block, and here was a big mercantile store, Wright & Beverley's, on the corner ahead of her. "Dealers in Everything," the painted sign above the second-story windows proclaimed. And there was the Long Branch saloon.

Having been told by someone that it was one of Dodge City's most prosperous establishments, she had expected something more pretentious. But it was like nearly every other business house along the street, crude and shabby and standing cheek by jowl with its neighbors on either side, though its front boasted rather more glass than some. Through the big windows and the gaping door, she could glimpse the interior—a long bar down the right-hand wall, tables at the back. The sun having now set, some coal-oil lamps were burning even though it was still a long way from getting dark. Male talk and

39

combined odors of whiskey and tobacco welled out to her.

Now that she had found the place, Emily could only stand in an agony of indecision. She had never in all her life stepped inside a saloon. No decent woman would. Yet every agonizing moment she delayed could bring Burl Channing on his own deadly mission to the Long Branch.

Just then, a pair of men left the bar and started for the door; they looked respectable, and Emily waited for them, her mouth dry. As they stepped out, she found her voice and made herself say, "Excuse me, please . . ." They gave her a glance as though they would brush by without pausing. Trying not to think about the idea they might have of her, she added hastily, "I'm looking for someone. It's very important!"

One of them went straight on but then turned and halted impatiently because his companion had hesitated. Emily plunged ahead. "Please, do you know a man named Frank Killian? I think he may be inside, or perhaps someone knows where I could look for him. But I can't go in that place myself."

"Killian?" the man repeated. "Runs the faro table?"

"That's what I was told," she agreed. "I'd certainly appreciate it if you'd give him a message. It could be a matter of life or death!"

For a second time, she was subjected to a stare that took her in from head to foot, but the man said, "Well, he's inside. All right—wait here. I'll tell him!"

"Oh, thank you!"

He turned back into the saloon; his friend gave Emily another scornful look and then, with an impatient shrug, went on alone.

Emily moved away from the door to where she could keep a watch up the street for any glimpse of Burl

Channing. She seemed to wait an interminable length of time. The man reappeared then to say, "He was just closing his game. He'll be out in a minute." Emily repeated her thanks and got another curious stare before the man hurried off along the echoing wooden sidewalk.

She looked around, and then a man she knew must be Frank Killian appeared in the doorway.

Chapter 4

Emily had no clear idea of what she had been expecting, but what she saw strangely impressed her. The man was well built, about the same height as Burl Channing but more slender and better looking. Since he was a gambler and from all accounts a successful one, it was natural enough that Killian would be well dressed, with a jeweled stickpin in his cravat—and he was a man who could wear one without its seeming out of place. He was smooth shaven except for sideburns; the tawny hair was beginning to recede at his temples. He would be, she thought, perhaps in his mid-thirties.

In that moment, as they looked at one another, his features were in repose, and she thought his rather hazel eyes held a look almost of calculation—the same expression they would have when he fanned open a poker hand or sized up an opponent across the table from him. One could hardly blame him just now for being suspicious, but after the first quick appraisal, she saw his expression change and become tempered with something she took to be admiration. He nodded as he said, "I was told it would be worth my while to step out and see who was asking for me, and plainly that was no mistake. I'm Frank Killian. Who are you, my dear?"

Full of the urgency of her mission, she said, "That isn't important."

"Oh, but it is!" he insisted, and then he smiled.

It was the smile that startled her. It seemed to soften the lines of his face and warm his eyes, taking all the aloofness from them. And it was the smile that turned her knees suddenly weak, for all at once there was a resemblance to her dead husband such as she had never seen in any other man.

She told him hastily, "My name is Emily Barker. I just arrived on the stage, down from Nebraska, with a letter my employer asked me to bring you. He said you knew him: Mister Jared McAfee."

"McAfee?" He nodded, but he looked surprised. Emily was already fishing for the envelope that had his name written on it; it was still sealed, though it showed some of the effects of being carried for three days in her reticule. Frank Killian accepted the envelope but didn't really look at it; his eyes were still on her, and it suddenly struck her that she must look very bedraggled indeed— her clothes crumpled and dusty, her hair out of control, like as not dirt on her face. It was all she could do to keep from putting up a hand to try to rearrange things.

If he had found anything wrong with her appearance, he gave no sign. He said, "You surely didn't come all this way just to deliver a letter?"

"Well, no. I'll be going on east with the next train— to Missouri."

"That won't be before noon tomorrow," he said with a pleased nod. "It gives us a chance to get to know one another. You'll let me buy your dinner, won't you?" He would have slipped the envelope into a pocket of his coat, but Emily exclaimed in protest and actually put a hand on

43

his arm to stop him.

"Oh, please!" she exclaimed. "I think you'd better read that at once—it's urgent! Because I have more to tell you." She looked around. "I feel terribly conspicuous, though—standing here like this. . . ."

Frank Killian seemed to understand. Without a word, he took her elbow and led her under the gallery of Wright & Beverley's—a sign hanging from it proclaimed it as "headquarters for cattlemen and drovers." The store was already closed and locked up for the evening, but its doorway was recessed, and the shadows there partly concealed them. So while Emily divided her attention between watching the street and studying the man's expression, Killian ripped open the envelope and took out the letter McAfee had written.

His face hardened as he read. He said nothing for a moment when he had finished. He slowly refolded the paper and tapped it on a thumbnail while he stood engrossed in his thoughts. He turned his glance to Emily then, and she saw its somber intensity. "Did you know what was in this?"

"Part of it," she said quickly. "Mister McAfee said it was to let you know a man named Channing was on his way, looking for you—to kill you! I'm not even sure he knew why. He was just very anxious that you should get the word."

"I'm a little surprised." Killian's voice held a dry edge. "I wouldn't have thought Jared McAfee would take that much trouble."

"He said something about being under obligations. He didn't explain what he meant."

"I don't suppose he would." The gambler shook his head. "This isn't a matter I feel like discussing—any of it: McAfee or Channing, either one."

44

She felt her cheeks grow warm in quick embarrassment. "Oh, I wasn't prying!" she protested. "Believe me! The only reason I asked you to read the letter is because I wanted to tell you this Burl Channing is here already. In Dodge!"

"What!"

"He was on the same stage with me from Nebraska. When he mentioned his name, I never let on I'd heard it— or had any idea what he was coming for."

Plainly, Frank Killian had been shaken by this news; it must not have occurred to him that the danger he was being warned against could already be closing in. He said now, "Maybe you can tell me: Just what does this . . . manhunter . . . look like?"

"You mean, you don't *know* him?"

"I never heard of him!"

"Well . . ." She searched for words to describe a man whom she had found quite normal—even attractive— until she learned who and what he was. "I'd say he was tall, rather dark—" Emily broke off with a gasp and clutched at Killian's arm. "But look! There he is!"

Killian turned quickly. Emily was glad now she had insisted on moving out of sight. With first dusk beginning to settle on Front Street, the shadows here under the gallery roof were deep enough to cover them as they watched Burl Channing approaching with a confident, reaching stride. She saw at once that he wore a gun and holster; he had the air of someone with business to perform who meant to lose no time in doing it. Emily glanced at the man beside her and saw the taut line of the gambler's mouth, the steady focus of his stare. He looked as though he were trying to memorize every line and movement of the approaching figure.

Channing halted in front of the Long Branch, looked

about him briefly, and then walked in. Emily exclaimed breathlessly, "He's looking for you. . . . Oh!" she cried in sudden alarm. "I can't stay here! I don't want to let him see me—let him guess what I know about him and what I've done!"

"Of course." Killian made a quick decision. "Come along!" He led her around the corner of Wright's on to Bridge Street. It was little wider than an alley, without sidewalks. A flight of wooden steps climbed the side of the store building, and there were barrels of trash set against the wall. Here they were out of sight of Front Street and the Long Branch; they faced one another in the rapidly gathering dusk, and still holding her arm, Killian said, "Don't be upset. Where are you staying—the Dodge House?"

"I suppose so. It was recommended. And my bag is there."

"It's handy for you, right across from the depot. If you want to avoid Channing, all you need to do now is go up a block to Chestnut Street and back to the hotel that way. You won't run into him at all." That said, Killian was silent a moment, studying her face in the dusk. "You know," he said earnestly, "I'm really sorry. I'd still like very much to buy your dinner—but as it is now, I'm afraid I can't even walk you to your hotel."

She herself was suddenly sorry. Other than her husband, she had never met a man who had so definite an effect on her; standing there close, aware of his hand at her elbow and of something in his voice and manner that stirred her directly, she asked in some anxiety, "What will you do?"

"I'll take care of myself," he assured her a shade grimly. Then his tone of voice altered again, and when he said her name, there was an intimate sound to it. "Emily, I simply don't know how to thank you! Except for you, he'd have come walking in on me just now. I wouldn't have been prepared, and I'd have been a sitting duck for him. I'll never forget this."

"You should thank Mister McAfee," she said. "It was all his doing."

"Of course—of course," he said, and again she saw his swift smile—Fred's smile—with a flash of strong white teeth. "I just wish you weren't leaving Dodge so soon. It means we won't have a chance to get acquainted—and I'll likely never see you again!"

She told him, "I just haven't any choice. I'm needed at home—my father could be dying."

"I see. I'm sorry." He freed her elbow and stepped away from her. "I suppose it's good-bye, then. Thank you again, Emily."

She left him, looking back once just before she turned the corner at Chestnut. He was still standing there watching her, and he lifted a hand in farewell.

When the woman had gone, Frank Killian stood looking after her briefly, but then, like a man pulled back to urgent concerns, he turned again to the matter of the stranger at the Long Branch. He moved up to the forward corner of Wright & Beverley's where he had a clear view of the front of the saloon. Emily Barker might have been startled if she could have seen the look of black rage that had settled upon him now, hooding his eyes and drawing his mouth into a tight line. In his hand was a short-barreled revolver that had appeared from its place beneath his coat. He waited while the dusk deepened along Front Street—distorting shapes and blossoming with the lamps going on in places of business all along this heart of Dodge City.

Killian held himself ready.

47

Burl Channing, entering the Dodge House with his own bag and Emily's, was puzzled not to see her in the lobby. He interrupted the desk clerk's excited talk about the holdup, but his question got a shake of the head. "Why no," the man told him. "Been no young lady in here, at least that I've seen."

Channing caught Wes Lowe's quizzical look. The gunman said dryly, "It would appear she's given you the slip. I noticed you hadn't been doing too well with her."

That got him a frown from Channing, who wondered if it had really been that obvious to the others on the coach. Without answering, he went and placed Emily's bag on the desk, asking the clerk, "Can I leave this here for Mrs. Barker when she does sign in?" The man stowed it under the desk.

Channing signed the register but shook his head at the key he was offered. "I won't be going up just yet," he said. He proceeded to open his own bag and take out a shell belt and holstered revolver, which he buckled about his waist. He closed and fastened the bag, telling the clerk, "If you'll keep this, too, I'll get it when I pick up my key."

Wes Lowe had watched all this, and now, as Channing turned to the street door, he said, "You going out? Maybe I'll just walk along with you a bit—I wouldn't mind stretching some of the kinks out of my legs." Channing was debating whether he would say flatly that he preferred not to have any company when a newcomer entered the lobby, the opening of the door letting in a brief burst of voices from the crowd gathered about the stagecoach.

The newcomer was a good-looking young fellow, strongly and stockily built, with black hair and mustache

48

and slate-gray eyes under heavy brows. He was immaculately dressed in a dark wool suit with a gold watch chain across the front of the waistcoat, a curled-brim derby set at a rakish angle. One would be much more apt to take him for a small-town dandy than for a man who had been a buffalo hunter and a professional gambler, who had taken part in the Adobe Walls battle against Quanah Parker's Comanches and was now sheriff of sprawling Ford County while still in his twenty-fifth year.

That he had come here looking for someone was plain in the way the man surveyed the pair from the stage, finally settling on Channing with a nod as he said, "Burl Channing! From Tug Wheeler's description, I was wondering if it wouldn't turn out to be you. Haven't seen you since that time a couple years ago, in the nations. Are you here on court business by any chance?"

Channing shook his head. "Leave of absence," he answered briefly. "My badge is in my pocket."

The newcomer was wearing his—a sheriff's star—pinned to his coat; two silver-mounted guns with ivory handles filled his belt holsters. He looked at Channing's companion. "If you were on the stage, then it must have been you who shot the holdup I just sent over to the coronerr."

Wes Lowe said coldly, "I didn't have much choice, sheriff."

"So the other passengers said." The lawman glanced around the lobby. "I thought there was supposed to be a woman. . . ."

Channing confirmed it. "Mrs. Barker. But she's not here."

"Well, that's all right." He turned again to Wes Lowe. "You're the one I wanted to talk to. Masterson's the name—they call me Bat."

"I had that figured," Lowe said.

"And you're Wes Lowe." Bat Masterson looked at Lowe, and they regarded each other with the wary respect of two men with similar reputations that might someday be a source of rivalry. Masterson said, "What I know of you fits the story I've been getting from your fellow passengers. They say you handled those road agents easily."

The other man shrugged slightly. "They were nothing much. Tramp cowhands likely pulling their first job."

"I don't recognize the one you shot. What can you tell me about the other one?"

Burl Channing answered that. "He was a yellow-haired fellow, medium height, with a bad case of peeling sunburn. His friend called him Dave."

Bat Masterson shook his head. "That doesn't register, either. Well, it's not surprising. There are plenty of horse thieves operating around Dodge. Come daylight, I'll send a deputy out to have a look around, though it's not apt to do much good. I've got a four-man staff and near ten thousand square miles of territory—Ford County and everything else, all the way to the Colorado border." He turned to Wes Lowe. "Right now I'd like you to come along to the office with me."

The gunman stiffened. "Why? You laying a charge against me for shooting a holdup?"

"No charge far as I'm concerned," the lawman said. "But you *are* the one that shot him, and the judge is going to want a statement. I'd like to have it taken care of."

Lowe seemed to accept that. He said gruffly, "Later, then. Just now Channing and me have other things to do."

"I'm afraid it'll have to be now. I never know how busy I'm apt to be later."

Masterson was being quietly insistent, and it was obvious to Channing the gunman didn't like it. He could see a real clash of wills developing over a point of slight significance. He thought to ease the sudden tension by suggesting, "How about a statement from me, Bat? Being an officer of the court . . ."

Masterson shook his head without looking at him. "It won't be needed unless the other testimony conflicts—which hardly seems likely." To Wes Lowe, he said in a tone that was more an order now than a request, "This is just routine. It won't take but a few minutes of your time. Come along."

For whatever reason, Wes Lowe was really angry; Channing almost expected to see him flatly refuse. But with a swing of his shoulders he turned toward the door, and the sheriff, starting to follow, paused to look pointedly at the gun in Channing's holster. "I forgot to mention," Masterson said. "The town has an ordinance against wearing firearms north of the deadline."

"Deadline?" Channing echoed.

"The Santa Fe tracks. It's a compromise: Dodge likes to encourage cowboys to enjoy themselves after a couple of months on the trail from Texas. But we can't have things getting out of hand. Long as they confine their celebrating to the South Side and don't let it slop over here where the town lives and does business, we don't figure to be too fussy. But there has to be a limit. And it has to be enforced."

Burl Channing looked at him squarely. "I hope you're not ordering me to take off this gun," he began.

"I wouldn't think of it!" Bat Masterson cut him off. "I'm a county officer—I got nothing to do with enforcing town ordinances. If you want an argument, don't raise it with me. Take it to the Dodge City marshal."

"Who, of course, happens to be—"

"My big brother Ed," Bat finished, a hint of amusement lifting a corner of his trimmed mustache. "You'll likely find him easier to deal with than me—everybody knows what a mean sonofabitch *I* am! But let me suggest"—he added a mild warning—"whatever your business in Dodge—even if it's legitimate—don't make us any trouble, Channing. Even if you have got a federal marshal's badge in your pocket!"

He smiled as he said it, but those cool gray eyes held a warning. Abruptly, Masterson turned to the door, and Channing saw that he limped slightly—that was permanent damage from a bullet in the groin taken during the shootout with Sergeant King a couple of years before in Sweetwater, Texas. Wes Lowe went, too, with no more argument, but the last thing Burl Channing saw before the door closed was the look of thunderous anger in the gunman's lean face.

It was out of the ordinary, he couldn't help feeling—such intense reaction over giving up a few minutes of his time to answer some routine questions and fill out a meaningless report. But Wes Lowe, like the sheriff himself, was clearly no ordinary man.

Chapter 5

As soon as he stepped inside the Long Branch, Channing knew his man wasn't there. It was early yet, and just at this hour the place was nearly empty. Channing entered a drab room, long and narrow, without windows, a few pictures on the walls, a set of longhorns mounted above the bar mirror. The tables and chairs at the rear were empty except for a man reading the Dodge City *Times*. The kerosene lamps had been lighted. A swamper with an apron tied about his middle was mopping up, kicking chairs around, while a bartender busied himself wiping glasses and lining them along the back bar.

None of these men looked as though they would be Frank Killian.

Channing left the door and walked over to the bar but shook his head when the man picked up a bottle and reached for a glass. "No, thanks," he said. "I understood you had a faro table working here."

"Why we do." The bartender seemed surprised to notice it was out of play. He called back to the swamper: "Joe, where'd Killian go to? Wasn't he here just a minute ago?"

Joe swabbed his wet mop across a patch of splintered floor boards. "Closed down his game and left. I heard him say he'd be back around eight."

"Well, there's not much action before then." The man told Channing, "Try later."

"Supposing I wanted to talk to this Killian—do you know where I'd find him? Where does he live?"

The question was relayed to Joe, who shrugged and said, "Hell, I dunno. Seems I heard he had a room at the Iowa House."

"And where's the Iowa House?"

"Next block," the bartender said with a jerk of the head. "On the corner." Channing thanked him and left.

The long spring twilight had ended, and full night was rapidly coming on. Lamps were burning now in buildings along the side street and yonder, across the Plaza. There, already, the evening was turning noisy with loud male voices and a woman's occasional shriek of laughter. Music drifted from one of the South Side's hurdy-gurdies. On the near side of the deadline, things were much quieter, although in this grainy dusk, sight and sound were both deceptive. As he emerged from beneath the shadowed gallery fronting Wright & Beverley's to cross the side street toward the dark bulk of the frame post office building, Channing thought he heard a whisper of movement close at hand and halted to investigate, touching his holstered gun.

Shapes were confused by the flight of wooden steps that angled up the side of the store building. If something moved in those tangled shadows, he couldn't be certain of it. Just then, a couple of men started toward him across the Bridge Street intersection from the direction of the post office. They were arguing about something, and whatever Channing might have heard in the nearby shadows was lost in the sound of their voices and a single spur chiming on the heel of one of them. Supposing he'd heard anything, it was likely a stray cat slinging through

54

the trash; so he told himself as he went on, passing the noisy pair and continuing along the line of buildings. A time or two in the next block, he thought he heard a furtive footstep behind him; but when he turned to look back, he saw no one. He put it down to imagination.

The Iowa House, on the corner of Third Avenue, was a good deal smaller than the more pretentious Dodge House hotel opposite the depot. In the tiny lobby, about the size of a postage stamp, a night clerk with patchy, unshaven whiskers admitted grudgingly that they indeed had a roomer by the name of Frank Killian. "But I don't think he's in. He works at the Long Branch; why don't you try there?"

"I just now did," Channing said. "They told me to come here. What's his room number?"

"Number seven—head of the stairs. But look! We ain't partial to people coming in off the street and bothering our guests—" At something in the look of this stranger, the clerk ran down. He stood nervously chewing the inside of a cheek as he watched Channing ascend the creaking steps.

The building wasn't very old—nothing in Dodge City was old, the town having been built just a half-dozen years ago when the Santa Fe laid its tracks past Fort Dodge—but the upper floor already had a smell of dust and of too many people. Approaching the closed door of number seven, Channing felt a tightening of tension. He paused to listen and distinctly heard a sound of someone moving about inside, the creak of a floor board. He knocked.

The sound ceased.

Channing waited a moment and knocked again. He said, "Killian?" There was no answer and no more sound of movement. He had a distinct feeling whoever was on the other side of that door was holding his breath. Channing had come too far, on too serious a mission, to be put off now. His jaw set. He lowered his hand to the knob, gently tried it, and felt the bolt slide; it wasn't locked. He drew his gun; with his left hand, he deliberately twisted the knob and let the panel swing open.

The light of a coal-oil lamp showed him the typical small-town hotel room—cheaply furnished, a brass bedstead taking up much of it, a wardrobe in one corner, a dresser and a straight chair and a rocker. The two windows ran almost from the carpeted floor to the low ceiling. At the foot of the bed, one hand tightly gripping the metal knob, the room's lone occupant stood staring at him. It was a woman.

Burl Channing lowered the gun without holstering it as he studied her. She was dressed for the street—and rather well dressed, Channing thought. She had jet-black hair, combed away from her forehead to a mass of curls, carefully arranged, at the back of her head. The dress, some rather shiny green material, was drawn in at the waist and fitted in a way to show off the generous swell of her bosom. Her earrings and necklace matched her dress. A beaded bag, a hat with a small bird fixed to it, and a wrap of some kind lay on the crazy quilt that covered the bed. She was definitely a good-looking woman, her natural coloring skillfully heightened, but just now she was staring at Channing with a pallor in her cheeks that made the rouge appear garish.

Her voice was steady enough—a throaty contralto. "What do you want?" she demanded sharply.

Channing told her. "I'm looking for a man named Killian. This is his room."

"No," she said.

"It's what I was told at the desk."

"They told you wrong." If she was afraid of him or more than momentarily startled, she covered it well. "Whatever name it was you just said, he isn't here. This is my room. You're welcome to leave."

It was a bluff, and she must have realized he knew it, but she put it boldly in a way he had to admire. Channing didn't argue, but neither did he leave. He stepped in, closing the door after him, and her cold stare followed him as he walked past her to the corner where the wardrobe stood. He opened it, revealing a man's suit and jacket hanging from the pole and a pair of high-button shoes. Closing the door, he moved next to the dresser and looked over the collection of articles beside the pitcher and washbowl: a long-shanked razor and soap cup, a pair of silver-backed military brushes, other men's items.

The woman said in the same controlled tone, "Just what do you think you're doing?"

Channing turned to her. "Shall we start over?" he suggested. "This isn't your room. There's not a thing that would indicate a woman lives here. Unless you use brushes like these," he added, taking one of them from the dresser, "and unless your initials are F.K." When she met his look with silent defiance, he dropped the brush back on the dresser and asked sharply, "Now—where's Frank Killian?"

He thought she wasn't going to answer; then she said sullenly, "I don't know."

"But you're expecting him. What's the fancy name for it—an assignation?" Her head jerked up. Ignoring her quick flash of anger, he went on coolly. "So obviously he won't be long. I'll just wait with you. Why don't we sit?" He indicated the rocker for her and turned the straight

chair around; he straddled it, leaning his forearms on the
back, the six-shooter loosely held in one hand.

The woman ignored his suggestion. She remained
standing, narrowly watching him; her color had returned,
but she seemed really alarmed to see him settle down for a
vigil. Suddenly able to contain herself no longer and no
longer trying to keep up her pretense, she exclaimed,
"What do you want with Frank? What are you—some
sore loser who's hoping to get back what he took from you
at the Long Branch?"

"I've never laid eyes on Frank Killian."

The woman didn't seem to believe that. "Then what
are you after?" Her voice rose, a strained note of hysteria
beginning to creep into it. "Who sent you? Is somebody
paying you? Damn you, are you here to *kill* him?"

Channing kept his own voice calm, trying to quiet
her. "You're jumping to conclusions—" he began. He got
no further.

Without warning, the door of the hotel room flung
open so violently that it struck the wall and rebounded; a
man's voice shouted, "Cora! *Drop!*" Channing's view was
hampered by the woman standing between. Hardly
thinking what he did, he flung himself sideways out of his
chair, and at the same moment, reacting to the order from
the doorway, the woman named Cora let herself fall to
hands and knees.

There was the briefest glimpse of someone outlined
against the opening just as a gun roared in a blast of
muzzle flame and room-trapped sound. On the dresser
directly behind Channing, the water pitcher went with a
smash as the bullet missed him. He had hit the floor
heavily, legs tangled with the chair when it went over. He
lay there, and he shoved his gun out ahead of him and

58

fired back. The two reports mingled deafeningly. A stinking fog of powder smoke rolled across the floor, blinding to Channing, who lay prone with his face against the carpet. Channing sent another shot after his first one and then managed a kick that freed his legs and disentangled him from the fallen chair. Without pause, he scrambled to his feet.

He didn't imagine his bullets had hit anything, but they had at least emptied the doorway. The man in the hall seemed to have lost his nerve after failing that first attempt. The woman—Cora—stared up at Channing from where she knelt. Satisfied she hadn't been hurt, he gave her no more than a glance and was on his way in pursuit from the room. As he cleared the door, that other gun fired once again from somewhere farther along the hall. He ducked and threw an answering shot. He heard running feet; at the end of the hall, a door banged open.

Following cautiously, Channing reached a turn in the hallway and saw the door standing ajar. Gaining it, he saw it opened on to the head of steps snaking down the outside of the building. Channing hesitated. Though he wasn't anxious to make a target of himself, the need to prevent his assailant from escaping sent him out onto the landing. The slot between the Iowa House and the building adjoining lay in total darkness except for light from a couple of windows. He dropped down a few steps, then halted to listen. He could hear nothing.

It was already too late. His man had vanished.

Burl Channing swore. It did nothing to relieve his disappointment and the aftermath of an experience that had set the adrenaline pouring through him. There was nothing to do then but remount the steps and go back down the hallway to Frank Killian's room. A door opened as he went by; someone looked out at him and at the revolver swinging in his fist, but Channing paid the man no heed.

The room was just the way he left it except that the woman had gone.

She'd wasted no time clearing out, taking away all proof that she'd ever been there—her hat, jacket, and bag; even the traces of the perfume she wore had been lost in the stink of burned gunpowder that the draft between door and open window was just beginning to dissipate. Channing looked about at the evidence of the brief gun fight—the smashed pitcher and the overturned chair. *So much for that,* he thought glumly. Remembering the gun in his fingers, then, he took a moment to punch out the used shells and dropped them into a pocket of his coat. He was replacing them with bullets from the loops of his belt when he heard voices and the trample of footsteps ascending the stairs from the lobby.

He had left the door open, and now, through the bannisters, he saw heads rise into view in the stairwell. The whiskered night clerk from the lobby was carrying on excitedly but letting another man come first; they were followed by several more, obviously pulled in off the street by the noise of gunfire. One or two of the hotel's guests who happened to be in their rooms emerged cautiously into the hall now to see what the excitement was about.

Channing gave all his attention to the tall man in the lead, the town marshal's star on his coat picking up glints of light from the corridor's one wall lamp. He thought he would have known Bat Masterson's elder brother even without the badge.

There was a strong family resemblance—the same gray eyes and heavy brows, the same air of competence.

But there were also differences: Ed was leaner, his face longer and less full, and there was an aggressiveness about Bat Masterson that seemed lacking in this older brother's manner and in the way he used his body. He came into the room, the night clerk close at his heels, and he looked around and then at Burl Channing, who had put up his gun and stood waiting to let the marshal of Dodge have the first word.

Ed Masterson said almost pleasantly, "It sounded like the battle of Gettysburg; I could hear it a block away. Johnson here tells me this room is where it happened."

"You don't see any dead bodies," Burl Channing said. "There's no blood—nobody hurt that I know of."

"But would you look at this mess!" Johnson exclaimed. Broken china crunched underfoot as he went to pick up a piece of the shattered pitcher.

"Put it on Frank Killian's tab," Channing said.

Masterson was looking thoughtfully at the stranger. "What's your name?" Channing told him, and he nodded as though the news didn't surprise him. "I kind of wondered. Bat was telling me about you not ten minutes ago. What happened here?"

"You mind closing that door first?"

The marshal looked around and saw the curious faces watching from the hall. He grunted. "We don't need an audience." Having stepped over to the door and shut them away, he said, "Now! You were saying—?"

"All I know," Channing told him, "is that I came up to this room trying to find a man named Killian. Instead, I found a woman. We were talking when the door flew open; there was a yell for her to get out of the way, and a gun opened up on me. Naturally, I shot back. I don't think I hit him, but the man was scared off. I chased him down the outside stairs, but he got away."

Ed Masterson was frowning. "Was it Frank Killian?"

"I don't know—I've never seen Killian. The clerk here said this was Killian's room. He didn't mention anything about a woman."

"I didn't know she was up here," the hotel man retorted. "Not till I heard you arguing. Then the guns started, and after that she came running down the lobby steps, white as a sheet and near hysterical. She went right past like she never seen me!"

Channing was curious. "Then you hadn't let her in? Or," he suggested, "maybe you're telling us she had her own key. That way, using the back stairs, she could come and go whenever it pleased her."

"So what if she did?" the hotel man said, shrugging. "It's none of the hotel's business, long as nobody complained."

"It's no secret," the marshal commented, "that Frank Killian was going around with Cora Tyler."

"Just who is she?" Channing wanted to know.

"Cora? Probably not what you're thinking. She's a singer—works for Ben Springer at the Comique, over across the Plaza. She's not a bad sort—and maybe I can understand what a woman like her sees in Frank Killian. . . ." He changed the subject. "You haven't told me yet," he reminded Channing, "what it was *you* wanted with him."

Burl Channing hesitated. "I don't intend to say anything more. Not here—not now."

For just a moment anger flashed in the marshal's steel-gray eyes, which so closely resembled his brother Bat's. But then he read the glance Channing shot at the night clerk, who was occupied in righting the chair that had been overturned during the gunfire. Masterson seemed to understand, for he nodded.

"There are better places," he agreed. "How about coming along with me, Channing?"

"All right."

Channing didn't greatly care if anyone got the impression he was being put under arrest. Under the eyes of Johnson and the half-dozen other curious men in the hallway, Channing and Masterson left the room and tramped downstairs to the lobby. Here and around the open door, they found more people who had been drawn to the racket of gunplay. The marshal told them that the excitement was over and no one was hurt and they should go on about their business. They accepted his advice reluctantly but moved off in a manner to indicate to Channing that Ed Masterson was well liked and popular with these men of Dodge City.

Outside, under the overhang of the gallery roof, a wooden bench stood against the front wall of the hotel, and the marshal indicated it. "We can talk here," he suggested. The two men seated themselves. The evening was mild for this early in spring. A faint wind brought the smell of the stock pens and of the river. Over across the Plaza, the noise from saloons and South Side dance halls came louder now as the night grew older.

Ed Masterson said, "You're making a problem for me, Channing. I hope I don't have to tell you, this ain't an easy town to keep under control. When the bulk of the trail crews start coming in any day now, it will really get lively around here. Policy has been to try and keep the rough stuff limited to the other side of the tracks where it can't do too much harm. Now you've gone and brought it over here, and strictly speaking, I ought to put you under arrest for breaking the law by wearing a gun north of the deadline. But," he added, "I'm not going to. For the time being, anyway."

"Thanks," Burl Channing said dryly.

"Don't thank *me*—thank your reputation with Judge Parker's court and the report I've had of you from my brother Bat. You're a federal marshal and, from all I've heard, a good one. It makes me think, whatever you're up to here in Dodge, you must have a good reason. But I think I have a right to know about it."

Channing was silent a moment. With some reluctance, he said, "I'll make it brief. Last summer, a man named Tom Nolan was murdered up at North Platte, in Nebraska. He was a stockman from Wyoming who'd delivered a beef shipment by rail to Omaha and had stopped off on his way home to look in on some people he knew. He was found in an alley one morning with his skull bashed in. The money was gone."

Ed Masterson looked at him in the faint light of the lobby window. "He was carrying it on him? Cash?"

"Almost twenty-five thousand, in a money belt. Tom Nolan didn't always use the best judgment," Channing admitted, "but he was a good man. He deserved better."

"You knew him, I take it."

"A little more than that." Channing's voice took on an edge of iron. "He gave me my first job at a time when I really needed it. That was in Illinois; he was a feed-lot man there. My folks had died when I was pretty young, and Tom became almost like my father. Later, he went out to Wyoming as the range opened up, got into ranching, and after a long struggle was starting to do well.

"I'd been out of touch, as a man will do. It wasn't until a few weeks ago that the word of his killing reached me—it was waiting for me at Fort Smith when I got in from a long stay in the field on court business. Soon as I could wrangle a leave of absence, I went up to Nebraska to see what I could find out, but after the better part of a year, the trail was dead cold. About all I could turn up was the name of a man who had been seen hanging around town with Nolan the night he died—a petty gambler, a no-luck tinhorn named Frank Killian. But Killian had dropped out of sight right after Nolan's murder."

Ed Masterson said, "Go on."

"Well, then I got a break. Someone showed up who had just come through Dodge. He knew Frank Killian and had spotted him running the faro bank at the Long Branch and looking like he was really in the chips—a far cry from the man who had been cadging drinks around the saloons in North Platte last summer."

"And because of that, you decided he was the one who did in your friend and stole his beef money?" The marshal shook his head. "That's not a lot to go on!"

"It wasn't enough to interest the local authorities in Killian or get a bench warrant issued," Channing admitted. "Tom had bought drinks for a lot of people that night. Others might have known about the money he was carrying. Still it was more of a lead than I'd had—enough that I thought it was worth my while to come down and lean on Killian a little, try to make him tell why he blew out of North Platte just when he did. At least, find out how much he might know about Tom Nolan's last night alive. And where it was Killian suddenly got his hands on the money to bankroll a faro table."

"And if he can't tell you that," Ed Masterson suggested quietly, "to your personal satisfaction—I suppose you think that proves him guilty of murder?"

"Marshal, I don't know what will happen. But I do know somebody tried to cut down on me just now. I can tell you now that when I was heading for this hotel, I had a strong feeling somebody was tailing me."

"But it don't add up!" the other man objected. "For it

to have been him, Killian had to know you were here and that you were after him. He had to have been *warned*! Is that possible?"

The argument stopped Channing. He scowled over it, with the night wind strengthening against the hard planes of his face. At last, he had to shake his head. "No, I guess it's plain enough. There's no way at all he could have got word."

"Then there you are! Will you let me tell you what I think?"

"I'm listening."

"I've had some occasion to keep an eye on this Frank Killian, watching how he runs his faro bank. He's a pretty cool customer—on the surface, at least. But with these professional gamblers, you never really know. Underneath, he could be on a tight fuse. And if Killian is a jealous man, finding somebody in there with his woman could have been all it took to set him off!"

It was logical, and it was convincing, and it had a devastating effect on the train of Channing's reasoning. But his jaw set. "You could be exactly right," he admitted heavily. "Just the same, I'm not through with Frank Killian! I'm not giving up the only lead I have—not after coming this far, not when finding Tom Nolan's murderer means every bit as much to me as it does to Tom's widow!"

They were quiet a moment, listening to the raucous drift of sound from across the Plaza. Finally, Ed Masterson stirred in his place on the hard wooden bench. "All right," he said. "I wish you luck. Had you been carrying a warrant, then Bat or me, either one, would have been glad to help you serve it. As it is, I'm afraid you're on your own. Out of respect for a fellow law officer, I'm not going to ask you to give me your gun in spite of the ordinance. You've been shot at once; you have a right to protect yourself. I just hope you'll try not to break any more of our laws than you have to!"

"I didn't come here to make trouble for you or for Bat."

"Let's hope not!" the other said a shade dryly. "Meanwhile, can I offer you a piece of advice?"

"Go ahead."

"You've worked hard, Channing, and you've made yourself a good reputation as a federal marshal. Why throw it away? How will it look on your record if you start off now on some private vendetta on no stronger evidence than what you have? How quick do you think you could *lose* that badge?"

Burl Channing's reply, when it came, was cool and crisply spoken. "I take this as being offered with good intentions," he said. "But I can't turn back from what I've started. I have a debt to Tom Nolan." Abruptly, he swung to his feet. "So good evening to you, marshal. I expect I'll be seeing you."

"Count on it," Ed Masterson said.

Chapter 6

Emily Barker was just signing the register at the Dodge House when she heard the shots—five of them, distinct and purposeful and run so close together it was clear more than one gun was firing. She had been half expecting this, and when it came, the steel-nib pen almost dropped from her fingers.

The desk clerk gave an exclamation and hurried to the door, leaving it open while he stared along the street. He hailed a passerby; Emily heard the indistinct sound of their voices, and then the clerk was back to report, "I was right! That was this side of the deadline! Not some cowpoke letting off a few, either. I wouldn't be a bit surprised if somebody got hurt that time!"

Emily had had a moment to regain her composure, but she had taken a shock, and her voice was unsteady as she said, "Does—does that sort of thing happen often here?"

"Often enough—though more often later on, after the shipping season really gets under way and the town is full of Texas trail crews. Even then, the marshal's men generally manage to keep it south of the Plaza.

"I got a hunch, though, about what we just heard. Just a feeling I had concerning that fellow who left your bag here at the desk for you. That Channing . . ." And he tapped a finger on the page of the register at the last signature above the line where Emily had started to write her name. In a strong, masculine script, she read: "Burl Channing—Fort Smith, Arkansas." The clerk explained: "He stood right where you're standing now, and I watched him strap on a gun, and I remember thinking to myself, 'This man intends to use it before the night is over!' Bat Masterson was here, and he reminded him about the town law. Bat seemed to know the man— said something about him being one of Ike Parker's marshals."

Suddenly, Emily remembered a sentence Jared McAfee had read from his letter: *I take it he's a lawman of sorts.* . . . She had puzzled over that, but the clerk's comment just now told her a lot. Back home in southern Missouri, she'd heard stories about the notorious hanging judge of Fort Smith, Arkansas; she remembered how incensed her father, a peaceable man, had been over the hard crew of marshals that brought outlaws from Indian territory to be condemned in Ike Parker's courtroom and hanged in job lots—five or six at a time—on the specially constructed gallows outside the courthouse. And so Burl Channing was a part of that! The news only strengthened her dislike of that strange, dark man whom she'd once found rather attractive until she learned he was the manhunter named in McAfee's letter.

To the clerk, she said only, "I don't really know anything about him at all. Mister Channing was just another passenger on the coach." She took the pen and shakily finished signing; afterward, she asked, "Do you know if I'd be able to get something to eat?"

"It's a little late," he told her as he handed over her

key, "but you could try the dining room. Cook may still have a fire going."

She spent a restless night, disturbed at the unexplained conflict between two men she had met only briefly and would probably never see again after she left Dodge on next day's eastbound. She couldn't help wondering about the exchange of gunfire she'd heard—wondering if it had meant what she feared and if she would ever know the outcome. She tossed and turned in her uncomfortable bed and listened to the nighttime sounds of Dodge City that came through her open window. Before morning, she managed to get some sleep and awoke in a calmer frame of mind.

After all, it was a situation she could do absolutely nothing about. She had come to Dodge with the assignment to deliver a letter; its consequences were beyond her control. Now she was needed at home, and in a few hours more she would be leaving.

Life was like that—full of unfinished stories in which a person becomes involved but never has a chance of learning how they finally came out.

So with her emotions in hand and her resolution firmed, Emily rose and dressed and prepared herself for another day of travel. She went down to the lobby meaning to inquire the exact time of the eastbound train's departure. Not finding the clerk at his desk, she decided to cross the street to the depot and get her information from the railroad agent.

The interior of the building looked familiar enough—a waiting room with uncomfortable benches, a space heater in a box of cinders, and a blackboard intended for train schedules but with nothing written on it. The only sound was the busy clatter of a telegraph key that rattled

70

on awhile and then fell silent. Emily waited, and presently the agent entered from the baggage room, carrying a sheaf of manifests. He saw her at the window and came over to give a perfunctory answer to her question: "The eastbound? Yes, ma'am. It pulls in at noon sharp; leaves at twelve-twenty—this is a meal stop. You want to buy a ticket?"

"That's right. I want to go to Springfield, Missouri."

The man pulled at his lower lip. "Best thing would be that I sell you a ticket to Wichita. From there you can make stagecoach connections by way of Joplin, so you don't have to go clear in to Kansas City."

"That sounds fine."

"One way?"

Emily hesitated only an instant before she nodded. "I don't ever expect to be coming back to Dodge. . . ."

He set to writing it up while she waited in a stillness broken only by the scratch of the agent's pen and the slow ticking of the wall clock. The telegraph key went into action briefly, then fell silent again. That reminded Emily of something Jared McAfee had said before she left North Platte, and as she paid with money from her reticule and accepted the long, thin ticket, she asked, "You wouldn't happen to have received a wire for me, I suppose? The name is Emily Barker."

"Barker . . . Well, let me think now. Does seem like—" He moved away, then came back with several yellow forms on a spike. He leafed through them quickly and gave a grunt as he located one buried part way down. "Yeah, I thought the name was familiar. This came two days ago." He ripped it off the spike and passed it through the grille to her.

Emily saw the wire was from North Platte, and suddenly her knees felt unsteady. She managed to thank

71

the man and afterward took her telegram to a bench against the wall before she attempted to make out the brass pounder's heavy scrawl. The message was from McAfee, and she read it through twice, making certain she understood it correctly:

> FURTHER WORD FROM YOUR SISTER STOP GOOD NEWS STOP YOUR FATHER'S INJURY NOT SERIOUS STOP NOW OUT OF DANGER

Suddenly, her tension and worry of the past week was broken in a rush, and Emily found herself shaking, almost unable to bear the unexpected sense of relief. With the telegram in her hand, she let her head fall back, and her eyes closed in a silent prayer of gratitude. She didn't hear the door open as someone entered the waiting room. A hand gripped her shoulder; a voice exclaimed, "Mrs. Barker!"

Her eyes shot open. Startled, she found Burl Channing standing over her. He quickly dropped his hand, but his face and his voice were anxious as he demanded, "Are you all right?"

"Why of course!" she said, puzzled and alarmed at the look of real concern that this man showed her.

But in the next breath his expression changed, became a cool mask. He said in brief explanation, "When I saw you sitting like that—and the telegram—" He indicated the yellow paper, then finished gruffly. "For a moment, I almost thought you might have fainted or something. I was afraid it had to be bad news about your father."

She hastened to correct him. "No, no. Just the

opposite, really. My sister says he'll be all right—he's no longer in any danger."

"I'm glad to hear it! From what you were saying on the coach, I knew how worried you were. This must be a real relief."

She admitted it with a wan attempt at a smile. "It's as though a great burden has been lifted!"

Channing continued to regard her closely. He said suddenly, "Mrs. Barker, I don't know if you've had your breakfast yet. I haven't myself, and I'm wondering if . . . maybe—"

Emily didn't let him finish. Her glance had fallen upon the holstered gun, and the sight of it brought back all her dark suspicions about this man; she said too quickly, "No, thank you."

She wished at once she hadn't been quite so abrupt. Burl Channing looked almost as though she had struck him. His head lifted, and his sun-browned face seemed to harden. He said stiffly, "Pardon me for intruding, ma'am. It won't happen again." And he turned to go.

Emily wondered at herself for what she did next. She was not a devious person, but suddenly it occurred to her this was an opportunity she shouldn't pass up. Encouraged to talk, he might give her answers to some of the questions that troubled her so. Added to this, confusingly, was a vague conviction that it had been wrong to speak quite so bluntly.

So there was a genuine note of contrition as she said quickly, "Wait!" and added, as he halted, turning: "I'm sorry, Mr. Channing—I really am. I didn't mean that the way I'm sure it sounded. I *haven't* eaten, and I'd enjoy your company. After all, I've known you longer than anyone else in Dodge City!"

"Fine!" he said. His whole manner had changed. He was smiling now with sincere pleasure; when she saw how her scheming had lightened the dark cast of his face, Emily all at once felt just a little guilty.

Except for an elegant name, the Delmonico had nothing particularly elegant about it; but in this raw frontier town it seemed a favorite eating place to judge by the many occupied tables. Emily and Channing had barely settled down and given their orders to the waiter when they heard a familiar voice wishing them a cheerful good morning. Jack Murtaugh descended upon them. The salesman appeared in the best of moods. He insisted on shaking hands with them both, and he said jovially, "Well! I'm happy to see we all survived our stagecoach trip—especially that unpleasant little ordeal right at the end of it. You know what I mean, of course."

"I think we know," Channing said shortly, and looked at Emily. But Murtaugh was not to be put off.

"I can tell you, that's the first time I was ever involved in a holdup—and I certainly hope it's the last! Well, at least we know one of that pair of cutthroats will never try it again! Nice work by our friend with the gun under his coat—you have to admire the way he drilled his man, dead center!" Murtaugh made a pistol of his fingers and aimed at Channing as he spoke.

One of Channing's hands, lying on the table, knotted into a fist. He said with studied patience, "Do you think the breakfast table is the place to talk about things like that?"

Unperturbed, Jack Murtaugh took hold of a chair back as he suggested, "Why don't I just pull this little ol' chair out and—" He interrupted himself, that idea forgotten as he glanced toward another table where a pair of men were seated. "Hey! Hold on! Right over there's the man I'm in town to see! Bob Wright's store is the most important establishment of its kind on the plains," he informed Emily confidently. "Be a feather in my cap if I can nail down a nice order from him! Think I'll just pop over and introduce myself. So long!"

And with that he was gone, on his way to the other table. Burl Channing said a little grimly, "There's a man with a hide three feet thick!" Emily, half amused, watched Jack Murtaugh bear down on the two men, breaking in on what looked like a serious talk. He went through the business of introducing himself; there were handshakes all around, and afterward Murtaugh proceeded to pull out a chair for himself and, plopping his elbows on the table, addressed his stream of conversation toward one of the men.

"I suppose you have to give him credit," she said. "At least he knows what he wants!" A moment later, she added, "The other man at the same table—has he got a *dog* under his chair?"

Channing smiled. "He has, indeed. You're looking at the mayor of Dodge—Mayor Kelley. His first name's Jim, but everybody calls him 'Dog' Kelley."

"To his face?" She looked at him in disbelief as he nodded and grinned. "And he doesn't get angry?"

"Not at all. He likes it. He was Custer's orderly when the Seventh Cavalry was stationed at Fort Hays, back a few years before the Little Big Horn fight. Custer used to keep greyhounds for racing, and Kelley had the care of them. Now he's got a bunch of his own; he's proud of his dogs, and he likes people to know it."

Their plates were served, and as they ate, Channing went on to explain something of the politics of Dodge City. Bob Wright, he said, had been a sutler at nearby

Fort Dodge; and "Dog" Kelley's saloon, the Alhambra, had been one of the first frame buildings put up when the railroad came through and this town was built back in 1872. Now, between them, they represented the established power in Dodge City government.

Emily scarcely listened. She was busy with thoughts of her own—and with questions she wished she had the courage to ask but didn't quite know how.

She was brought out of these concerns as a newcomer approached their table—a stockily built man whom Channing proceeded to introduce to her: "Bat Masterson is the sheriff here." The lawman accepted the chair he was offered, placing his derby on his lap. Emily felt the weight of his cool-eyed stare as Masterson realized who she was. "You're the one I wanted to talk to last evening, Mrs. Barker—about the holdup. But when I got 'round to it, you seemed to have disappeared."

Under the lawman's steady regard, she felt her cheeks grow warm. "I'm very sorry! After everything that had happened, I'm afraid I didn't feel like talking to anyone." The excuse sounded lame even to her own ears.

"Well, it's no matter. I got a full report without having to bother you."

Burl Channing asked, "Lowe made his statement?"

The sheriff nodded. "Though he did seem pretty much put out—and I still don't know why. Anyway, the matter's on file. The dead outlaw is on his way up to Boot Hill, and I've circulated a full description of the one that escaped. I'll be heading out directly to have a look at the place where it happened, but there's not much likelihood of picking anything up."

Emily's curiosity was prompted by something Masterson had said. "It's true, then? Here in Dodge City, you actually call your cemetery 'Boot Hill'?"

Bat Masterson's full mustache lifted to a wry smile. "A bad joke, isn't it? But there it is! A half-dozen years ago, when the town was new, there was quite a lot of killing. Twenty-five men died with their boots on that first season alone, and they had to be put down somewhere— in a hurry! Well, we're not quite *that* wild any longer; I mean the city council has plans for starting a regular civilized cemetery for respectable citizens who'd as soon not be buried alongside gunmen and drunk trail hands and tinhorn gamblers."

He turned to Channing. "I've had a talk with my brother Ed—about that little run-in you had last night and the things you told him afterward."

Channing's dark face looked just then as if it might have been carved from stone. He said bluntly, "So?"

The sheriff shrugged. "I just wanted to put in a word on my own: I suggest you watch your step. Ed is easy-going—but push him too far and he can be tough. And if not him, there are others who might."

"Meaning you, Bat?" Channing suggested quietly.

"I mean that I think a lot of Ed. That's all I'm saying."

Emily felt her breath catch in her throat while she watched these two men, their faces nearly expressionless, eying each other across the litter of the breakfast dishes. After a moment, Burl Channing looked thoughtfully at his coffee cup as he turned it in the saucer. He lifted his eyes again to the other man. He said, "I'm in town to do a job, Bat. I intend to get it done."

"I see. Well . . ." Words seemed to have gone as far as they could. Bat Masterson got to his feet, derby in hand. For a moment, he considered the other man, who remained seated. He turned then to Emily Barker, inclined his head, and said, "Ma'am." After that, he was

77

gone, moving off through the tables to the street door.

Emily was left completely bewildered; she sensed that deadly, important things had been said or hinted at, but as far as she was concerned, these two had been talking in riddles. She looked at the frown on the man seated across from her—he seemed almost to have forgotten her presence.

Suddenly, she could hold back no longer. Into his silence, she asked, "Is it true you're a federal officer from Fort Smith? One of Judge Parker's marshals?"

Slowly, Channing lifted his head; his stare had coldness in it. After a moment, he spoke. "You said that as though you thought it wasn't a good thing to be. . . ."

She made herself meet his hard look. She said with a flash of stubbornness, "You can't deny the stories about that court. All those hangings!"

His eyes, intent on her face, flickered suddenly—it was almost as though she had insulted him, and she all at once felt abashed at the words she had spoken. But they couldn't be taken back, and she had to return his look and feel his anger. Then he lifted his shoulders.

"I've only two things to say to that," he told her in the gruff manner that seemed to be habitual with this man when his emotions were roused. "First, I'm only an officer of the court. I go out in the field and serve warrants and make arrests—I have nothing at all to do with holding trials or passing sentences."

"I understand that."

"But even so," he went on in the same clipped tone, "I think Ike Parker is right more times than he's wrong. And I might remind you, so do the higher courts. His judgments are almost never reversed on appeals. The authorities know a dirty job has to be done if there's to be any control over those vermin that infest the Indian nations!

"Do you have any notion of the kind of men we deal with down there? They're the scum of the frontier— renegades, stock thieves, army deserters, killers. . . . Personally, I think the worst are the ones that exploit the Indians by peddling snake-head whiskey to them—pure poison, unfit to drink. You just don't handle that sort with kid gloves! As I say, it's a dirty job—but somebody's got to do it."

"Still, does it have to be you?"

She had said it without thinking how it might sound. He frowned. "Meaning, I must like it, or I could quit? Well, if that's the way you see it—" he said, and finished with a shrug.

Emily bit her lip, thinking that she was getting nowhere with this. But she could not give it up without a try at least at the question that chiefly bothered her; she took a breath and asked, "Are you here in Dodge City on court business?"

"What?" The question seemed to take him by surprise, but he shook his head and answered briefly, "Oh, no. It's a personal matter." And the way he said it— closed up and final as though he would say no more— convinced her of her failure.

Chapter 7

They walked back to the hotel together, saying little. On the porch, Channing faced the woman for a moment of awkward farewell. He said, "Your train leaves at noon?" And when she nodded: "Well, then I guess I won't be seeing you again." He made a move to offer his hand, changed his mind, and took off his hat with it instead. He worried the brim, turning it in his fingers as he thought of all that he should be saying if he could have found the words. "I hope your journey home is a little pleasanter the rest of the way," he managed. "And that the news will still be good when you get there."

"Thank you. I've really stopped worrying since that telegram."

He felt she had something more she wanted to say, something that really seemed to trouble her, but in the end it went unspoken, and Channing could think of nothing himself. "Well—good-bye, then," he said, and he turned abruptly and left her. He didn't look back.

He was bitterly angry at his inability to talk to this woman. The aversion toward him that he sensed in Emily Barker had been enough to throw him completely off his stride. Her coolness to him had been clear even before she learned of his connection with Hangin' Judge Parker's court. Apparently, she chose to see him as a person who liked violence—a surly-tempered man, not simply one who had trouble expressing himself to her. Besides that, he was by nature reluctant to share his personal affairs with anyone.

Well, and what of it? Emily Barker would soon be gone. Yet he knew it was not going to be easy to forget the admiration he'd felt for that spunky, attractive young woman at their very first meeting in front of the stage station in Nebraska.

He was in this reflective mood when, retracing his steps, he met "Dog" Kelley coming from the direction of the Delmonico, the greyhound padding along beside him.

The mayor of Dodge was not a particularly impressive character—a dumpy figure, eyes heavy lidded, full cheeked, mouth almost hidden under the fall of his mustache. He halted in front of Channing and demanded, scowling, "Do I know you, mister?"

"We've met once. I'm not exactly a stranger to Dodge. The name is Channing."

"Dog" Kelley glanced meaningfully at the holster. "Then I suppose you know you're breaking the law, wearing that gun."

"I have permission," Channing said. "Your marshal gave his okay for reasons he can explain. Why don't you ask him?"

"I mean to!" The mayor was obviously displeased. "I can't see much point passing ordinances if there's to be an exception made for every single Tom, Dick, and Harry— but I'll let it go for now. I figure I can count on Ed Masterson to know what he's doing."

"I would," Channing agreed shortly. He would have passed on, but "Dog" Kelley wasn't finished.

"No problem figuring," he said gruffly, "what George Hoover and Ham Bell and some of them other law-and-

81

order boys would say about this. All they need's an excuse. They'd like the town run like a church. Well, I can tell you there's no prayer meetings being held over there south of the Plaza—and while I'm mayor, there's no point expecting it. Hell, this is Dodge City! The boys have always come here looking for a lively time, and I say they got a right to find it. Because if they don't, they'll take their business somewhere else."

Channing was skeptical, hearing the familiar argument. He thought, *They'll go wherever their boss knows he can find a railroad and a buyer to give him the price he wants for his herd.* But he wasn't going to argue with a man who could order his gun lifted if he took the notion; and just at that moment there was a diversion.

A rattle of hoofbeats and a thin chorus of yells turned them both to look across the Plaza, where shadows of spring clouds flowed before a brisk stir of wind. A string of riders, a dozen of them, had burst into view out of the clutter of buildings that made up the South Side. Anyone who had ever seen a bunch of Texas cowboys freed from the monotony of the trail and riding into a cattle town with pay in their pockets would know that these cowpunchers had just crossed the long wooden bridge across the Arkansas and were on their way to make their presence known in Dodge.

"Dog" Kelley lifted a pointing arm. "There you are! One of the first crews of the season. Starting now, we should see business really beginning to pick up. Like I told you—they always come back!"

"Like robins . . ." Burl Channing muttered dryly, but the other apparently didn't hear him. If these were harbingers of spring, they were noisy ones. They came at a gallop, and there were shouts and laughter, and now a couple of the riders unlimbered belt guns and began

82

punching bullets at the clouds overhead. The shots cracked flatly and bounced off false-fronted lifts of buildings along Front Street and served to bring the street to life.

Doors slammed open. "Dog" Kelley's hound started barking. The mayor swore at him to shut him up and then headed for the corner of Bridge Street with the animal at his heels to intercept the riders. Yonder, Channing glimpsed the town marshal, Ed Masterson, hurrying across the dust with the same intention. He was just as happy that it wasn't up to him to convince these high-spirited riders they should obey the posted signs by taking off their guns and depositing them at the first saloon they entered.

Meanwhile, he was back where he had started in his search for Tom Nolan's murderer. He turned and went on along Front Street to try again at the Long Branch.

In her room, Emily Barker was nearly finished packing—moving almost mechanically, her mind a prey to confused thoughts and feelings. The knock that came at her door brought her back. "Yes?" she called. "Who is it?" Hearing no answer, she went and opened the door and stared. "Why, what on earth are you doing here?"

"I got your number from the register," Frank Killian said. "Please, may I come in? Just for a moment?" He was as neatly and impeccably dressed as he had been the first time she saw him, his lean cheeks freshly shaved, but it seemed to Emily he was under strong tension. Once again, she saw in his face the disturbing reminder of her dead husband; not thinking of anything to say, she simply stepped back, and he entered, closing the door behind him. "I hope you'll forgive me, Emily," he said, his manner deeply serious, "coming here like this."

She found her voice. "I'm afraid I don't understand. . . ."

"Of course you don't. But I had to see you—at least once more. Since those few minutes in the dusk last evening, I haven't been able to think of anything else. And now, in an hour or two, you'll be gone."

"I've bought my ticket," she acknowledged.

He nodded and laid his hat on the chair. "I know. I saw you coming from the depot; you were with Channing."

"Why yes—I was. I didn't see *you*."

"Naturally, I kept out of sight." He added quickly, "Oh, I'd never hide from Burl Channing—and I'll never run from him! Believe me, if there has to be a showdown, I'm ready for it!"

"Last night, I heard shooting," Emily said. "I was terrified! I couldn't help but think for a moment—"

"That he'd found me?" Killian shook his head, with a flash of the smile that was so like Fred's. "No, nothing like that. Though, except for the warning from you, it would have happened."

"Thank goodness it didn't!"

"I'm sorry you had to worry about it—and yet, for selfish reasons, I guess I'm glad, too." He touched her arm briefly, let his hand drop again. It made her aware of how close they stood, and she turned and moved away a few steps, working at her uncertain feelings as she looked from the window into Front Street and the Plaza.

Standing there, she saw a group of riders burst into view down at the lower end of Bridge Street and come on at a gallop, rebel yells sounding thinly across the morning, a couple of handguns firing random shots. She'd heard stories of the noisy way Texas trail crews liked to hit a railroad town at the end of the long drive.

She heard the man move up behind her. "So this

84

morning," he continued, "I watched you and Channing go into the restaurant and later come back to the hotel."

Emily turned. "You must have been *spying* on us!"

"Not spying—just hoping for a chance to see you alone before your train left and it would be too late. Worst of all, while I waited, was having to wonder what sort of things he was saying about me. Filling you with lies, of course. Even—" His eyes grew suddenly hard. "Even something about a woman, I wouldn't doubt!"

"A woman? Why no!" she exclaimed, then wondered why she felt she had to defend Burl Channing. "There was nothing at all like that. In fact, he never mentioned you— not even when I asked point blank just what he was doing here in Dodge City. Actually, that was the main reason I agreed to have breakfast with him," she went on. "I thought it could be helpful to you if I was able to learn something about his plans."

"You wanted to help me?"

"Of course. But I'm afraid nothing came of it. Except for one thing that was new to me: Mister McAfee said Channing was some sort of lawman, but I'm not sure if either of you realize the man is a federal marshal."

Frank Killian's eyes narrowed a trifle when he heard this. Emily hastened to add, "But he also told me he's here on personal business, nothing to do with his job. That's absolutely the only hint he would give me." She shook her head. "I'm sorry I wasn't able to do better."

"You've done fine," he assured her. "Especially for someone who had to be kept in the dark about the meaning of all this."

Emily lifted a hand in protest. "Please don't think I'm prying again!"

"Of course not. But on the other hand, after all you've done—all I can tell you myself is what was in

McAfee's letter. It seems I'm accused of a killing, one I didn't do and know nothing at all about. In other words, the whole thing's a stupid mistake!"

"But—if that's so, can't you reason with this man? Explain to him?"

"Reason with *him*?" Killian's voice turned to iron. "You've seen what he is! Emily, look at me!"

He took her by the shoulders, turned her so that she could see his lean and handsome face full in the light of the window. "He calls me a killer," Frank Killian said harshly. "But which one of us carries a six-shooter even though he knows it's against the law? And which one will be believed, no matter what kind of lies he tells, just because he's a federal marshal—and I'm a gambler!

"I won't apologize for what I am," the man went on, his voice vibrant with feeling. "Everybody in the West is a gambler when you come down to it. It's the only way of life here, whether he has the guts to stake everything on a turn of a card or relies on the gun in his holster or on the market for Texas cattle. When his luck is in, a man rides high, and when it goes down, he goes down with it. A man like me knows all about that—better than most. Just as I know now, Emily," and his grip on her shoulders tightened, "that from here on my luck, for good or bad, is bound up in you!"

"Me!" She stared into the eyes so close above her own. "You can't know what you're saying! Why we've only just met."

"And if we hadn't," he reminded her, "by now I could be a dead man!"

"But all I did was bring you a letter," Emily protested. "And I was paid to do that. Oh, no—you're very wrong, Mister Killian. There's nothing special about me."

"There's everything special!" A thought shadowed Frank Killian's eyes then, but he met her look directly as he offered a blunt confession: "I'm no saint; I wouldn't pretend I was. I've known plenty of women but none like you. None that could ever mean anything to me like you do. That's the plain truth, Emily . . ."

Suddenly, he pulled her to him, his arms going about her; then his lips were on hers. She made a wordless protest and tried to break free, but the arms were much too strong. Her own arms went up, her hands moving to the man's broad chest—and it was then she discovered a lump of hardness beneath Frank Killian's left arm and knew it was a gun in a hideout holster. . . . Despite herself, she was reminded fleetingly of his scornful words a moment ago when he contemptuously accused Burl Channing of carrying a weapon. But could she really blame Frank Killian for looking to his own protection? His life was threatened.

She seemed to surface from a deep submersion then; her senses returned, and she turned her face away, gasping a little. She had her hands against Frank Killian's chest, and when she tried to push him away, he released her. She felt flushed, and her heart thudded. She tried to speak, but the words were lost.

Killian trapped both her wrists in his strong hands. "Remember what I said!" he cried. "You're my luck! A man like me always knows his luck—who knows better? And if you should go, my luck goes with you. Don't do it, Emily! Don't leave on that train at noon. You can't!"

She tore her eyes from his, feeling the pounding in her temple. She managed to say hoarsely, "I don't think you had better stay . . . here in my room . . . any longer!"

Killian seemed to know it would be a mistake to press her further. After another moment, he said, "All right," and her hands were freed. She stood and watched him turn from her to the door, taking his hat that he had dropped on the seat of the chair. He opened the door, cast a glance into the hallway, then looked back at her for a final word.

"Don't go!" he asked once again. Then he was gone, and Emily silently closed the door.

Chapter 8

Early as it was, the Long Branch had only a few customers. The swamper was busy at his usual thankless task of keeping the filth of spilled liquor and tobacco juice off the floor, kicking a slop bucket along as he swept his wet mop around in wet, gleaming arcs. He shook his head before Channing had time to ask his question. "No, Killian never has shown up—last night or this morning, either. If it keeps up, Chalk Beeson's going to get sore and want somebody else in here running his faro table. It don't make no money being shut down!" Chalkley Beeson, in conjunction with a man named Bill Harris, owned and ran the Long Branch.

The swamper appeared a good source of information, and Channing put a question he'd been wanting to ask someone: "Supposing I was to run into him, what manner of man is this Killian?"

"You mean what's he look like?" The swamper leaned on his mop and ran the flat of a thumbnail through beard stubble, screwing up his face to think. "Like a gambler is all I'd know to say. Cocky sonofabitch, flashy dresser. Reckon there's women might even think he's what they'd call a handsome sort of stud."

Burl Channing wanted to protest. Could this possibly be the same Frank Killian who had been described to him

89

any number of times, as he had been last summer in the bars of North Platte: a loser, a down-at-the-heels tinhorn who slept in his clothes and cadged drinks? The answer was: it had to be the same! Moreover, there had to be an explanation for the way such a man could turn suddenly prosperous almost overnight. In Channing's mind, there was no longer much doubt that he was closing in on the man who had murdered Tom Nolan for a belt stuffed with cattle money.

He thanked the swamper and turned to leave when he saw Wes Lowe leaning his elbow on the bar and finishing off a schooner of beer. The gunman had been watching; he saluted Channing with the glass, saying, "Wait up." Channing paused beside him, and Lowe said, "You appear to be looking for someone."

"You could say that."

The gunman's look weighed the urgency of his manner. "Buy you a drink?" he suggested, but Channing refused—too early, he said. Lowe said, "Just a minute, then, while I finish this one." He drained it off, studying the other man above the schooner's rim.

Setting the glass down, Lowe wiped his mouth with the inside of a sleeve. "None of my business, of course. But this man I just heard you asking about—Gilman?"

"Killian . . ."

"Whatever." Lowe accepted the correction. "You sound as though you're having trouble locating him. Is it important?"

"Important enough."

"Well, I've got some time to kill. Maybe I could lend you a hand. Dodge isn't exactly a big town; between the two of us, it might not take too long running him to ground."

Burl Channing's eyes narrowed slightly. He almost

found himself asking, *Do you always take this much interest in other people's business?* But he left the thought unspoken. He was in a poor temper; already this morning he had come close to quarreling with Emily Barker, with Bat Masterson, and with Mayor Kelley himself. It was time he got his bad mood under control. He told the other man, "Thanks, but I guess I don't need any help. As you say, it's not that big a place. If Killian is around, I ought to be able to run him down."

The gunman shrugged. "Suit yourself," he said, and swung back to the bar. Channing considered him for a moment. This offer had surprised him, but he knew by now that Wes Lowe sometimes did unpredictable things. He turned away and left him.

Walking out of the saloon, Channing passed a couple of newcomers entering, with jingling spurs and the smell of the trail on their clothing. They were talking loudly with the unmistakable drawl of Texas. They were part of the newly arrived trail crew, of course, ready to see the sights of Front Street. More cowpokes were grouped in front of Wright & Beverley's. Channing didn't see any guns; apparently, there had been no trouble for Masterson to get this bunch to obey the ordinance and give up their weapons. He wondered how often it proved to be that easy.

The tiny lobby of the Iowa House was deserted, and he went on up the stairs, to find the door of number seven standing open. As he approached it, he saw a woman at work, cloth tied around her head. She was singing and bustling about, using a feather duster; a mop and broom leaned against the doorjamb. She interrupted the hymn she was nasally intoning to answer his question impatiently: "Ain't nobody in this room. Man that was staying here moved out."

"Mind if I look?"

She shrugged a shoulder. "You won't see nothing!" She went on with her work. Channing went over and opened the clothespress. It was empty; the suits and other garments that had been there the previous evening were missing, and so, he discovered, were the personal items from the dresser. The drawers, as he expected, held nothing at all.

The woman demanded, "You through nosing around? Or do I have to call the manager?"

"I'm through. When did everything get moved out?"

"I wouldn't know. Before I came to work. I was told the room was empty and to clean it up. I just do what I'm told and mind my own business." She went back to her chores, grumbling as she swept up shards of the smashed water pitcher. Channing left her.

He could picture Killian waiting to make sure the coast was clear before coming up the back stairs again to hastily gather his possessions. Short of laying a trap in the man's hotel room, Channing didn't see how he could have prevented Killian's moving out.

So much for that. It seemed about time that he had another talk with Frank Killian's mistress. . . .

The Comique, on Maple Street south of the deadline, where it faced the open expanse of the Plaza, was another box of a building much like any other in Dodge. There were the usual bar and tables, but what mainly distinguished the Comique and gave it status as a "theater" was the small, curtained stage at the back of the main room. There was a brief row of footlights behind tin reflectors, and an upright piano stood to one side. When Burl Channing entered, the place was doing little business as yet; a half-dozen men sat drinking at the tables, and a baldheaded bartender was at his station, busy cleaning glasses. Cora Tyler stood by the piano as she and a seedy-looking accompanist went over a piece of sheet music.

So she actually was a singer—it wasn't merely a fancy name for prostitute. She had an untrained but not unpleasant voice. It was a voice that could hold its own against the hubbub of a noisy nighttime crowd. Listening to Cora sing, Channing shook his head at the bartender and walked back toward her; he moved slowly, taking this opportunity to study the woman while she was still unaware of him.

She was a little older than he thought the previous evening. She was more plainly dressed now, but she had been and still was a handsome woman. All in all, he was willing to accept Ed Masterson's judgment—that she wasn't a "bad sort." Preoccupied with singing, Cora appeared not to notice Channing until he was within a few yards of her. When she happened to glance at him, she abruptly stiffened, and her voice broke off. The piano player went on for another measure or two before he noticed, followed her stare at the newcomer, and let the music die.

Channing nodded greeting. He reminded the woman pleasantly, "We didn't finish our talk."

"Yes, we did." Her rouged lips closed tightly.

"I disagree. You'll remember, we were interrupted." Seeing her continued hostility, he was moved to add, "Actually, I'm sorry about last night—particularly, the way you got dragged into it. I'd like to apologize for that." He looked around, indicated an empty table. "If you'll let me buy you a drink," he suggested, "and give me ten minutes, I'll try not to bother you any further."

The intention to refuse showed in the cold flash of her eyes, but something stopped her. He suspected she was curious; also, she probably wasn't used to being apologized to, and that must have had its effect. In the end, she told the piano player, "We can do this some other time, Harry. Thanks." Harry slid off the stool and headed for the bar. Cora called over, "George, bring us a couple of glasses."

The bartender had been looking on, scowling suspiciously and probably hearing everything that was said. He caught up a bottle in one hand, the shot glasses in the other, and came around from behind the bar as Channing and the woman took their seats. George set the glasses in front of them, filled them, and stood waiting while Channing brought out a couple of coins in payment. These were scooped up in a broad fist, and the man left with another cold look at Channing.

Neither Channing nor the woman touched their drinks. She folded her arms on the table and looked at him, waiting. He tried to soften the hostility in her manner by commenting, "I liked your singing, by the way. As much as I heard of it."

The attempt failed. "You've got ten minutes," she reminded him in a chill tone.

"I won't waste them." Speaking quietly, he got directly to the subject. "I didn't get what I came looking for in that hotel room yesterday."

"I told you then—"

"You told me a lot of things we both knew weren't so. You've got a voice that carries; as I found out later, you were heard clear down in the lobby. I thought you might be on the edge of hysteria. Now it strikes me you were really trying to give Frank Killian a warning and let him know there was somebody in the room with you. You could have got me killed—if he'd been a better shot or hadn't lost his head and run when he missed me the first try." He added dryly, "You'll probably say it's too bad he missed!"

Again, she shrugged, not denying anything. Channing went on. "When I got back to the room after chasing him, you were gone. And this morning, so is he—taking everything with him. That means I have the job of finding him all over again."

"I heard he left town." Cora Tyler threw that out with an air of not caring whether he believed it or not. He didn't. Channing shook his head.

"Killian wasn't on the morning stage," he pointed out, "and the trains haven't been through yet. Besides, he's had a good thing going here in Dodge. His luck's been running for him; why would he deliberately turn his back on it? The man's a gambler. I think he'd lie low and gamble on waiting me out."

The woman said, "That's *your* gamble. You can please yourself."

Burl Channing told her, "Waiting games aren't my style. That's why I'm here talking to you."

She pushed out her lower lip; her dark eyes met his in defiance. "It won't do you any good!"

"You're certainly not going out of your way to make matters easier! But the only thing I'm after just now is to get a message to him. Will you deliver it? You're the logical one to do that—"

"You think so? And supposing I knew where he is," she retorted. "Why would I do you any favors?"

Channing met her look squarely. "Why? Because otherwise I'll just have to go hunting for him. His clearing out the way he did suggests he had another place he could run to. Under the circumstances, I've got a fair idea where it is.

"I hold no grudge against you, Miss Tyler—believe

me, even after last night. Unless I'm forced, I really don't want to drag you into this. All the same, in a town this size, it shouldn't be impossible to find out your address."

The woman's face had gone white; her eyes blazed with anger. She said through tight lips, "You're a bastard!"

"When I have to be," he acknowledged. "I'm sorry."

They had been holding their talk down, neither of them particularly interested in being overheard by the rest of the room. Still everyone must have seen the woman was angry; and now George, the bartender, let his voice break across the stillness, saying harshly, "Channing, you've had your ten minutes!"

Channing turned his head as the man brought up a sawed-off shotgun and clattered it on the bar. Channing looked at the weapon and then at the bartender's threatening scowl. He observed, "You know my name."

George shrugged thick shoulders. "Hell—the whole town knows you by this time. But let me just remind you: you ain't in Indian territory now. Ike Parker's badge, that you carry, don't mean nothing in Dodge—and it means even less here south of the deadline!"

"You may have noticed, friend," Burl Channing replied coldly, "that I'm not wearing it." But he didn't argue with a shotgun. The time he had bargained for was, in fact, used up. He got to his feet, replaced his chair beneath the table, and looked again at Cora Tyler, who hadn't moved. Knowing that he had every eye on him, he said to the woman but also to the room in general:

"My message for Frank Killian is simple enough. I came to Dodge City for a reason, and I won't be put off. He's tried once to ambush me and had to run for cover when it failed. Now if he's any kind of a man, I expect him to come out of hiding and meet me face to face so we can settle the business I have with him. He won't like it if I have to come and dig him out! " Channing looked around the room.

"I hope somebody will tell him that for me," he finished crisply. Then he turned and passed down the length of the room through a silence that was broken only by the sound of his own boot heels. As he left the Comique, he knew that, one way or another, it would not take long for Frank Killian—and with him probably all of Dodge City—to get word of the challenge.

Chapter 9

Both of the daily trains through Dodge City, eastbound and westbound, passed the depot at midday within an hour of one another. Today, Burl Channing made it a point to be on hand, ready to make sure no one answering the description of Frank Killian should board either one without his knowing and to take steps to prevent it.

He was on the platform when the earlier of the two makeups, heading west for Colorado, came thundering in with drive wheels shaking the ground and bell clanging.

He paid little attention to the passengers who alighted from the two coaches for their dinner stop at the Dodge House, but no one got on without his close survey. Later, as arrival time for the eastbound drew closer, a rather larger contingent of travelers began to straggle up and collect along the platform, carrying their luggage; again, Channing watched closely, constantly alert, and for a second time was satisfied that Killian hadn't tried to escape from him by way of the railroad.

But when the hum of wheels on steel rails faded off along the Arkansas Valley and the crowd of station loafers began to disperse, Channing found himself with a nagging question. For there was one person he had expected any moment to see board the cars, and for some reason it hadn't happened. He was chewing on this puzzle as he crossed the rutted width of Front Street. He had just mounted the steps of the Dodge House when the door opened, and Emily Barker herself stepped out. He had never seen her look so pretty or so fetchingly dressed.

An April wind, carrying the smell of rain, swept against them as they halted there on the porch of the hotel. Channing blurted out, "Mrs. Barker! I'm afraid you've missed your train!"

By now, he never knew whether to expect her to speak to him or to brush on by as though he didn't exist. This time, however, she acknowledged his concern with a nod. "I know," she said after the slightest of hesitations.

"But I thought you had your ticket, that everything was arranged."

"Well, I—" She seemed uncomfortable under his regard. She hurried on: "At the last minute, I knew I couldn't go—not yet. There are things that have to be settled—decisions I have to make."

"Decisions?"

"Yes. About myself, about what I really want to do. Since I got the word that my father's going to be all right—well, the pressure to go just isn't there anymore. I'm not needed at home now, and yet if I go back, I may find myself trapped. I'm not ready to face that. I need time to make up my mind about the future and—oh, a lot of things. However much time it takes."

"I see."

But he really wasn't sure that he did. He had a strong impression she was holding something back—that she hadn't told him her real reasons for staying in Dodge City. Because of the long-standing coolness between them, he didn't feel free to ask any more questions; nor could he

obey the impulse to tell her, *I'm very glad you're staying!*
Instead, he merely nodded and said, "Good luck, then."
And he stood aside to let her descend the steps past him.
He stood looking after her as she turned down Front
Street.

The decision not to use the ticket she had bought was
something Emily couldn't even attempt to explain—
certainly not to Burl Channing, hardly even to herself.
She only knew that after that moment in her room with
Frank Killian, there was no way she could turn her back
on the situation she found herself involved in. Meeting
Channing just now had only reminded her of her confused
feelings. He and Frank Killian were the elements of a
puzzle that wouldn't let her rest until she came to terms
with it.

And so she had let the eastbound pull out without
her, and now she moved along Front Street, embarking
on the course she had set for herself.

She tried to ignore the stares she got from the Texas
trail hands and soldiers from Fort Dodge she passed on
the block west of the hotel. She didn't have to be told a
woman was considered bold to venture on Front Street
like this by herself, but that couldn't be helped—hers was
a case of necessity. A gust of wind threatened to disrupt
the careful effort she'd put into fixing her hair and
clothing as attractively as possible. But when she reached
the entrance of Wright & Beverley's, she paused and was
able, working blindly, to anchor the hairpins more
securely and push the coils into better shape. She
straightened her skirt, set her shoulders defiantly, and
stepped inside.

It was larger than Jared McAfee's store in North

Platte, and it seemed virtually stuffed with merchandise—
a clear justification of its reputation as the most important
mercantile establishment on the plains of western Kansas.
With an experienced eye, Emily made a quick survey as
she moved among the loaded bins and counters, the
stoves and kerosene lanterns, guns and saddles, hats and
boots and stacks of clothing, both male and female. There
were a number of customers in the place, but Emily saw
no other women and suspected they were something of a
rarity. A clerk, catching sight of her, came forward to ask,
"Yes, ma'am. Can I help you with something?"

"May I speak to Mister Wright, please?"

"I'm afraid he's busy just now."

Following his glance along the crowded aisles, Emily
caught a glimpse of the man Burl Channing had pointed
out to her that morning at breakfast; the storekeeper
seemed occupied with a salesman, being shown the
contents of his samples case. "It's all right," Emily said. "I
can wait."

"That's up to you," the clerk said, impatient with her
now that he knew he didn't have a sale. "I'll tell him." He
moved off, leaving her alone.

Fighting nervousness, she occupied herself with
studying the store's displays and mentally making note of
prices, comparing their markup with McAfee's and her
own father's place in Missouri. She became absorbed in
this and was taken by surprise when Bob Wright appeared
beside her to say with cool politeness, "You want me to
help you with something? We claim to sell anything from
a packet of pins to a portable house!" He eyed her as he
said it with male awareness. He was hardly a handsome
man. In his late thirties, with a prominent nose and a jaw
that receded under a drooping mustache, he had a level

eye and a self-assured manner that probably came of knowing he was the most affluent businessman in this booming cattle town.

Emily hastened to introduce herself and to explain, "I didn't come in to purchase anything. As a matter of fact, I'm looking for a job."

His manner became instantly cooler. "A job? I'm sorry, Mrs. Barker. You can surely see we have no ladies here. As a matter of fact, Front Street isn't generally thought of as fitting for a respectable woman alone."

"I'm afraid I can't help that," she said. "I hope I'm respectable, but I *am* alone; I really need the work. Besides, looking over your stock, I'm sure you must have a good many women customers."

"Indeed we do. But—a female sales clerk?" He firmly shook his head. "I never heard of such a thing!"

Emily had by now overcome her initial shyness. "Then isn't it about time?" she insisted, warming to her argument. "Who but a woman can really help another one decide what she wants to buy? And I'm a very good salesman, Mister Wright!"

The merchant looked at her. He said dryly but with a certain amount of admiration, "I'm beginning to suspect as much!"

"And I also know bookkeeping," she went on. "So I can help with the accounts—with billing and invoices and correspondence—anything of that nature. Believe me, I've had years of experience. Just recently, I left a job with Jared McAfee's Mercantile at North Platte in Nebraska—"

A new voice broke in. "By golly, that's right, Bob. McAfee himself was telling me only the other day when I was up there working that North Platte territory what a peach of a lady bookkeeper he had and how much he was going to hate losing her." Emily looked around in astonishment and saw Jack Murtaugh, sample case in hand—she hadn't noticed it was he Bob Wright had been talking to when she came in. The fat man went right on, his booming voice rolling through the store: "And, Bob, didn't I hear you say something about trouble keeping your accounts up to date?" He beamed at Emily. "Well, sir, here's your answer—made to order."

The merchant was plainly weakening but was still reluctant to break with a male-dominated tradition. He said stubbornly, "I don't know. A business establishment just don't seem the place for a woman!"

"She suited Jared McAfee—and *there's* a real, solid businessman for you. He wouldn't steer you wrong."

"I can do the work, Mister Wright," Emily insisted, "if you'll give me a chance."

"What have you got to lose?" Jack Murtaugh insisted, pressing hard. "So maybe she can't unload barrels and crates. You've got men working for you who can do *that*—but can any of them balance a cash book?"

The other man gave in. He scowled as he asked Emily, "When can you start?"

"Any time at all. Whenever you want me."

"In the morning, then? Eight-thirty sharp—we open at nine. We'll give it a try for a week."

"Thank you!" she said. "I promise you won't be sorry," she added as Wright nodded curtly and walked away through the cluttered aisles. Emily turned to the fat man. "And thank *you*, Mister Murtaugh! You were the one who made him change his mind. . . ." She hesitated before she went on, careful to keep her voice lowered. "But—I just can't remember seeing you at the store in

103

North Platte. Did you really discuss me with Jared McAfee?"

"Never met the man," Jack Murtaugh admitted blandly. "But I couldn't see how it would do any harm putting in a word for a fellow traveler. Anyone'll tell you Jack Murtaugh likes to help out when he can. Glad you got the job. Hope it will work out for you."

"Oh, I know it will! I won't let you down—I really am a good bookkeeper. And thank you again!" She shook his plump hand.

"No trouble at all," Jack Murtaugh assured her. But he sounded puzzled as he added, "I thought someone told me you were in a hurry to get to Missouri. On account of your pa being hurt. . . ."

"You're right, I was. But I've had word that he's in no danger now, and—well, I just don't really know what I should do next. I want to take time to decide—and meanwhile I have to have some money. My funds are getting low."

He said, "Then I think you're doing the right thing." He abruptly changed the subject: "It's quite a story, isn't it, about that fellow Channing—the one we came down on the stage with."

"What story?" she demanded quickly. "I hadn't heard anything."

"But I saw you in the restaurant with him this morning. I took it for granted you knew all about it." Jack Murtaugh shrugged chunky shoulders. "Anyway, what I heard was, he and some local—a gambler—were involved in a shooting in a hotel room last night. Because of a woman, they tell me. And now Channing's put out a dare for the other fellow to come out and finish the thing in the open. The whole town's waiting to see what will happen—

just itching for a fight. Well, I've always been told Dodge was a lively burg!"

He seemed blandly unaware that he had filled her with horror and dismay.

Channing had offered his challenge, and now he let it have its effect. The rest of that day he spent making himself visible along Front Street. He knew perfectly well that Frank Killian would have heard of his dare long before this; Channing's confident presence could only serve to rub it in and make it impossible for the gambler to avoid a confrontation and still save face. Channing kept his own counsel, saying little to anyone but making it plain that he would wait indefinitely for Killian. The pressure was on the gambler, and it was certain to grow.

He had his evening meal at the Delmonico and afterward walked the few steps to the Long Branch. There had been a couple of showers during the afternoon that left the street pocked with puddles and turned the sunset into a murky pileup of clouds the color of a bruise.

In a chair in front of the Long Branch, he found Wes Lowe enjoying a cigar and looking over the town. The gunman gave him a nod and a pleasant "Good evening." After a brief exchange, he went on into the saloon, wondering, not for the first time, if some definite purpose had brought the gun fighter to this town and just what he was finding to occupy his time. To Channing, Wes Lowe remained an enigma.

Lamps were burning in the Long Branch, and a poker game was in progress at one of the rear tables; the faro table was still conspicuously closed. He ordered a drink at the bar and let it sit while he deliberately rolled a cigarette, taking his time, with the air of someone under no pressure. A man he thought to be Chalk Beeson, owner of the Long Branch, was standing at the end of the bar in conversation with the bartender. Beeson didn't look too pleased. Pawing at his heavy mustache, he demanded loudly, "Ain't you had any word from him today? Any idea whether he means to be in this evening and run his table?"

"No word at all, Chalk," the bartender told him. "Nobody I've talked to has seen hide or hair of him since yesterday afternoon."

The saloon owner swore. "I dunno how he expects either of us to make a profit on a game that's closed down. If Frank don't want the concession, I sure as hell can find someone who does!"

Burl Channing fired a match and got his smoke going. His impassive face showed little trace of the satisfaction he felt from what he overheard. Frank Killian was beginning to pay a price by staying out of sight.

Someone sang out a friendly greeting as Ed Masterson came in off the street. The marshal, plainly a popular man, acknowledged the hello. He spotted Channing and came over to the bar, shaking his head at the bottle in the bartender's hand. He was all business. He told Channing without preliminary, "I'd like you to do me a favor."

"If I can."

"This is Bat's concern, but he's not in town right now. Thing is, I just got word Ham Bell is holding a man who answers the description of the one that got away after the stage holdup yesterday. Bat said you thought you could identify him. Would you take a look?"

"I suppose," Channing said. "Where is he?"

"Ham's got him at his livery. I sent one of my men to help hold on to him while I decide whether to put him

106

under arrest or let him go. We could step down there now if you're willing."

"All right."

Channing tossed off his drink, and they walked out into the early twilight. Bell's big livery barn was over on the south side of the Plaza, handy to the toll bridge so punchers off the herd grounds could put up their horses as soon as they hit town. The two men angled across Front and set off down Bridge Street to walk the three blocks to the barn. It was still fairly quiet even on the South Side; it would take an hour or so for the evening to tune up.

Ed Masterson said, "You've really stirred up the animals! All I been hearing today is talk of how you've called Frank Killian out—and bets as to whether he intends to show."

"So far nothing's happened," Channing said. "I don't even know, for a fact, he's still in Dodge."

"The betting seems to be that he is." They walked on a moment in silence before the marshal added, "Let me just remind you, I got a stake in this. 'Dog' Kelley don't like it that I've let you hang on to your gun for self-protection. If you deliberately go and provoke a fight, I may have to make it my business."

"I haven't said anything about a fight. All I want is the man to come out in the open and deal with me—on what terms is up to him. I can't help what the town might be trying to make of it."

Bell's livery was a wooden barn with stalls enough to accommodate a sizable incursion of riders into Dodge City. An oil lantern burned above the runway; Ham Bell himself met them as they approached the wide door.

"Where is he?" Ed Masterson wanted to know.

"Your deputy's got him in the office." Bell was a spare figure of a man who held himself sternly erect. He treated the marshal with proper respect, although Channing knew they belonged to different political camps—Hamilton Bell being of the "law-and-order" faction that considered Mayor Kelley and Bob Wright and their policies much too lax for a town like Dodge.

The office door stood open; the deputy, a man named Nat Haywood, leaned against a rolltop desk, keeping watch over the prisoner, who sat sulking on the edge of an unmade cot. Bell said, "Well, there he is. He brought a horse in a half hour ago. Seemed like he could be the one Bat said to keep an eye out for."

The deputy put in, "I can see a bandage under that shirt—looks sure enough like a bullet burn."

Ed walked over to the cot, plucked the hat from the prisoner's head and dropped it beside him. Light from the desk lamp shone on untrimmed yellow hair, on surly features that were scabbed and scarred by a bad case of peeling sunburn. "That's him," Burl Channing said. "He's one of them that held us up. His partner called him Dave."

The prisoner, squinting back at him in the glare of the lamp, was weakly belligerent. "He's crazy, or lying," he declared gruffly. "I never held up nothin'!"

"No question he's the one," Channing said. "There's others who were on the stage can also identify him. Show him to Wes Lowe—he's the one shot him in the arm and killed his partner. He'll have no trouble identifying him."

"That's good enough for me." Ed Masterson replaced the towhead's battered hat. "On your feet," he ordered. "I'm jailing you on suspicion. When the sheriff returns, you'll be turned over to him."

"What about his animal?" Bell asked.

"Give my brother the bill. The county will settle it."

The prisoner had to be hauled to his feet and marched out between the two lawmen, complaining at every step but not showing any actual resistance. Burl Channing followed them. It was only a few hundred yards to the city jail across the Plaza and this side of the tracks, just opposite the depot. He watched them go and then paused for a long look over the flat stretch of river bottom and the Arkansas River, lying like beaten silver under a colorless sky. It was almost full dark now except for the lantern at the livery entrance. After a moment, he turned and started in the direction of Front Street.

He had walked only a dozen yards along the uneven surface of Bridge Street when he heard a boot-sole crunch on pebbles close at hand. That was all the warning he had. Next moment, they were on him.

They came in a silent rush—at least a half dozen, he thought in the first confused instant, but it quickly shook down to three. Channing tried to sidestep as he reached for his gun, but it was already too late; someone struck his arm, and the weapon leaped from his hand. The number of his assailants told against them; amid pantings and cursings and jostlings, they got in one another's way. A face rose before him—there was enough of a gleam from the barn lantern to show it was a narrow face, with heavy brows like a continuous black slash. Channing struck out, and that one dropped, leaving him with sore knuckles where they had bounced off a bony skull.

Next moment, a weight fell across his shoulders; an arm crooked itself about his throat from behind and cut off his wind. He doubled forward, trying to dislodge and hurtle the man across his back; instead, he was borne down to his knees in the street mud. There was a ringing in his head now as he fought vainly for air. With an effort, he managed to buck against the weight pressing on him and somehow broke the hold. Gasping, he dragged cool air and a smell of stale sweat into his lungs. Then something that had to be a gun barrel struck his head.

His hat cushioned its impact, but the blow was solid enough to send a swirl of stars across his vision. He swooped into blackness and recovered enough to find himself lying on his face in the mud, incapable of movement. Just above him, a voice he thought he knew yelled something, and a gun went off twice. After a confused sound of retreating footsteps, everything stopped. Channing lay dazed with pain throbbing in his skull.

The voice spoke again. He had not been mistaken— he did know it. Ed Masterson asked anxiously, "Are you all right?"

"I think so."

Moving carefully, Channing rolled over so he could get his hands under him and try to push himself up. The lawman cautioned him, "Better go easy!" He took his time, nursing the steady throb of his skull. He got himself into a sitting position and gingerly felt the lump on the back of his head. It was painful, but his fingers found no blood.

A couple of men came hurrying from the direction of the livery barn. A lantern carried by a hostler swung its circle of light along the ground; the other man was Ham Bell, who exclaimed, "What's going on, marshal?"

Masterson indicated the hurt man. "Channing here was just set on by a bunch of thugs. I saw them sneaking around and left the prisoner with Haywood while I came back to see what they were up to."

"Lucky for me you did!" Channing admitted.

"Which way did they go?" the liveryman wanted to know.

Masterson said, "Toward the river. I counted three altogether. Never got a good look at them."

Ham Bell swore. "This is why I say it's not enough just to keep things quiet up there on Front Street! We need a big enough police force so a man can come down here across the tracks on legitimate business without taking his life in his hands!"

It was an old controversy, and the marshal didn't rise to it. "It looked to me they bent a gun barrel over his head," Ed Masterson commented. "I think he should be got to a doctor."

"No," Channing objected. "I'm fine."

Bell said, "You don't look it," but he insisted on climbing to his feet, using the hand the marshal reached to help him. At the effort, pain exploded inside his skull, and the world spun about him. As it settled in place again, he was aware of a faint taste of blood in his mouth.

Just then, there was another arrival. Coming down from Front Street, Wes Lowe had heard the shots, and he hurried forward as he spotted Burl Channing in the glow of the lantern. Channing made introductions and told the man briefly what had happened to him. He shook his head when Lowe asked, "Did you recognize anyone?"

"There's human rats in some of these alleys," Ham Bell said darkly, "that wouldn't hesitate to knock a man in the head on the chance of finding the price of a drink!"

Channing had a different idea, but at the moment he preferred keeping it to himself. The hostler, looking about with the aid of his lantern, had found his hat and his gun and handed them over. Channing put the weapon in its

111

holster and kept the hat in his hand rather than try to draw it on to his aching head. He thanked Masterson again, and after some more inconclusive talk, the thing broke up.

Wes Lowe fell in beside him as Channing started again for Front Street. "You sure you can manage? Maybe I'll just walk along with you."

"I'm all right," he insisted for perhaps the twelfth time. After they had gone a few yards, he found his legs alarmingly unsteady but hated to admit it. There was a wooden fence to their left, and he said, "Maybe I'd better sit a minute. I'm shaky yet. . . ."

He half sat, half leaned against the fence, waiting for his strength to return and for the pounding in his head to ease. "You'd better watch yourself," Wes Lowe cautioned him. "You could have a concussion—if nothing worse!" He added, "I figure Ham Bell was mistaken. Those three weren't just after the price of a drink!"

"No, they weren't," Burl Channing said.

"It looks plain enough—they were trying to fix it for this Frank Killian so he wouldn't have to face up to the dare you threw at him. It's going to come as a blow when he learns they failed! The town's going to be interested now to see what else you two cook up for each other."

Something in his tone made Channing lift his head sharply, skull-splitting pain almost forgotten. As they faced each other in the night that had settled over Dodge, he said coldly, "I don't want you to think this is just a sideshow put on to amuse you *or* the town! It happens we're dealing with a murder."

Lowe echoed the word in a tone of apparent surprise. "Murder? Nobody told me that!"

"Well, now you've been told."

112

A moment later, Channing tried his legs again. They walked on toward the lights of Front Street with a silence now between them.

Chapter 10

Emily was laying out the clothing she would wear for starting work next morning when she heard Frank Killian's knock. This time, she recognized it at once. She hesitated, and when the knock was repeated, she laid aside the blouse she had been holding up to a small mirror; she took a breath and went to open the door.

Killian seemed in a strange, almost euphoric mood. He closed the door behind him and stood looking at her with eyes that shone in eagerness and with that flashing smile that touched a core of weakness somewhere inside her. "You didn't go!" he exclaimed. "I begged you not to—and you didn't! I knew you couldn't just pack up and leave, not when you knew how much it meant to me!"

"You may be interested to know," she said, "I have a job now. I begin tomorrow at Wright and Beverley's."

"That's even better!" he exclaimed. "It means you're serious about staying."

"I don't really know how long yet," she put in quickly. "But while I'm deciding, in any event, I need money to live on."

"Well, you're here now; I won't look further than that. Emily . . ."

His arms reached to draw her to him. But she was too unsure of herself to trust letting herself be kissed—not by

114

him, not just then. She turned her face away, saying faintly, "No! Please!" She thought he wasn't going to let her go, but then his arms dropped away, and she stepped back. "Please!" she said again, not meeting his eyes. "I told you I have to make some decisions. And—this isn't helping!"

When he didn't speak at once, she looked at him and saw that he had sobered. His high spirits of a moment ago had faded. He said, "I don't understand. I thought I'd made it clear enough how *I* feel."

"I know." She made a small, helpless gesture with one hand.

"Then what's wrong?"

Under his urging, she knew she had to answer. She tried to settle her breathing. "It's just—there's so much I don't know about you!"

She thought his voice took on an edge. She could hardly be surprised if he was resentful. "What do you want, the story of my life?"

"Yes, I think I do—eventually. Just as you have a right, sooner or later, to find out whatever there is to know about *me*." She faced him, then, determined to have it out. "I know one shouldn't listen to rumor, but I admit I'm bothered by something I heard today."

"From Channing?" He spoke the name with tight lips.

"No, not from him. He's never told me anything at all. It's just . . . talk, that in spite of what you told me, you and he did have some trouble last evening. What's more, that there *was* a woman mixed up in it. A singer was what I heard. . . ."

His look rested on her for a long moment while she felt the weight of his anger, but when he answered, he seemed disappointed. "You're bound to hear anything.

And I can't stop you from believing it. I told you already, I won't pretend to be a saint. But as far as other women are concerned, anything of that sort was over the moment I met you. It's the truth, Emily. That you *can* believe!"

The sincerity and warmth of his answer were most convincing. "I don't doubt you, Frank. Honestly, I don't!" Still there was more, and she had to have it out. "But what about another rumor that says Burl Channing has sent you a challenge to meet him tomorrow? From what I hear, the town seems to be betting that you won't do it."

That stung him. She saw it in the way his head lifted, his mouth pulling tight at the corners. "They say that, do they? They think I haven't the nerve to face him?" But then his whole manner changed. The stiffness went out of him, and his mouth quirked as he said almost smugly, "Why, then, I'll just have to prove them wrong, won't I? If he's still around by tomorrow."

"Do you have any reason to think he won't?"

"Oh, almost anything can happen. That's always true." But though he said it lightly, she had an odd feeling just then that she could not put a name to.

"And if you do meet tomorrow," she persisted, "what will happen?"

"That's up to Channing."

Suddenly, she felt remorseful over the prying questions she had been throwing at him; she laid a hand on his arm as she said earnestly, "Frank, if I've upset you—I'm sorry! Somehow I've never felt more unsure of things. And I've no one else to turn to."

"Of course." He covered her hand with his and gave it a reassuring squeeze. "I don't want to pressure you. I'll

116

leave you alone now—there'll be plenty of time for us later. I'm glad you've made up your mind to stay, for a while at least. I'll do all I can to keep you from changing it." He leaned, kissed her swiftly, and gave her hand another squeeze.

After that, he had his hat and was turning to the door. He had swung it open and stepped briskly into the corridor when Emily saw him freeze and heard his muffled exclamation. She looked past him across the lamp-lit corridor. A man stood with both hands pressed against either side of a closed doorway; he leaned there with his head dropped forward against the panel and his hat on the floor at his feet.

The man was Burl Channing.

Emily exclaimed, "What's wrong with him?"

"Dead drunk, obviously!" Killian's tone held so much hostility that it drew her glance; when she saw the malevolence in his scowl, it shocked and startled her—in that moment, he looked almost ugly. She glanced quickly away.

"I don't think he's drunk," she protested. "He looks ill—maybe hurt." So saying, she went to him, speaking Channing's name. She could not say whether he heard her. He didn't move from his odd stance, braced there with feet spread as though otherwise he would crumple to the floor. But the light from a wall lamp touched his face and confirmed her guess. His face was not flushed from alcohol; it looked slack, with a strange pallor.

She saw the key thrust in the lock—having somehow mounted the lobby stairs, he had managed that much before strength failed him. Emily turned it and pushed the door open on the darkened room; she said, "Now, Mister

Channing, I'm going to try to help you. Put your weight on me." She wasn't sure he heard. She ducked under his arm, then took the wrist and brought it down on to her shoulder while she slipped her free arm about his waist. She urged him, "Try to walk. . . ."

Somehow they made it—he seemed aware enough to partly help himself, or she would never have been able to hold up his solid, muscled weight. The light from the hall showed a gleam of brass that directed her toward the bed. She got him there and swung about so he could lower himself to a sitting posture on the edge of it. He was breathing heavily, and she thought she heard him mumble something; then, slowly, he folded sideways. She lifted his legs and got him stretched out on his side, unmoving.

Frank Killian, who had stood by, entered the room and, fumbling about on the commode, got a match struck and lit the wick of the kerosene lamp; its yellow glow smeared and steadied as the chimney clinked into place. Emily said across her shoulder, "Bring that over here, please." In the direct glare of light, she studied the man on the bed. There was something wrong, she thought, at the back of his skull. She touched the place, felt the swelling, and exclaimed, "Why he's been hit there—hit hard! I wonder how in the world it happened!"

And then something made her turn slowly to Frank Killian.

He stood beside her, staring at the man on the bed, with the light of the lamp he held casting his features into strange contours. She heard herself say in an odd voice, "I hope *you* don't know anything about this. . . ."

Killian's head jerked about sharply. "What do you mean?"

In confusion and despair, she cried, "I don't know what I mean! I—I don't understand anything that's going on! I'm sorry. . . ." She added urgently, "Could you get a doctor up here to look at him? I'd feel better if we knew just how badly hurt he really is."

"All right," he said, and returned the lamp to the commode. "I'm not sure I should bother except that *you* ask me . . ." At once, he was gone, not waiting to hear any thanks.

Afterward, alone with Channing, Emily stood and looked at him for a long time and wondered what she could believe and what she really felt where he was concerned. Seen like this, off guard, defenseless, and without his brusque manner that she found so hard to penetrate, he looked utterly vulnerable; she had to admit there was something likable in this man. There were even hints of kindness, such as those she'd glimpsed when he had been concerned for her during the stage journey or in the morning at the depot when he misread her reaction to the telegram about her father. These things simply didn't jibe with the image of him as a ruthless and relentless manhunter on a mission he stubbornly refused to explain.

No less than Frank Killian, Channing was a puzzle in contradictions; she did not know really how she felt about either one of them. . . .

Sooner than she expected, Killian came back with the doctor in tow. A gray-haired, efficient man, little inclined to speech once he had given his name as Clevenger, the doctor worked swiftly, checking the hurt man's pulse, listening to his breathing. He examined the swelling on Channing's skull and pulled down the lids of both eyes with his strong, bony fingers. Unable to contain herself, Emily demanded, "Will he be all right? What can you do for him?"

"Not much anyone can do, really," he said. "He was struck with something, and fairly hard. The skull doesn't appear to have been damaged. He may have some concussion, but it doesn't show in the pupils. The best medicine is just to let him rest and see how he is in the morning."

"Should someone stay with him?"

The doctor shook his head. "I don't see much they could do."

She said, "My room is just across the hall. I'll look in from time to time just to make sure."

He agreed that that was a good idea, and in a few minutes he was gone, leaving instructions to keep him posted should there be any change. Shortly afterward, Frank Killian left as well, his manner distant and uncommunicative.

The night passed uneventfully, and once Emily satisfied herself that Channing didn't really need her attention, she was able to get some rest. She was up early and was leaving for the first day on her job when she heard stirring in the room across the hall. She knocked, heard Channing's gruff answer, and looked in at him.

He was seated on the edge of the bed; his color was better, and he looked clear eyed but perplexed to see her. Emily hastened to explain: "You were in pretty bad shape last night—I'm not even sure you knew what was going on. So we got you into your room here and made you as comfortable as possible."

"'We'?"

"Yes—the doctor and I." She couldn't bring herself to mention Killian or admit she actually knew and had frequently met the man Burl Channing was hunting for. She went on to report what Clevenger had told her. "He said you may have a concussion. You seem to have taken a really bad blow on the head—"

"I know I did." He didn't elaborate, but by now she had learned this man seemed almost incapable of discussing his personal affairs with anyone—at least with her. He merely said, "I remember coming up the stairs and getting out my key, but after that, things are hazy. I don't know what I actually saw and did and how much I only imagined. But if you're the one who looked out for me, then I appreciate it!"

She passed over that. "The doctor hoped you might be feeling better by morning—and it appears you are."

He touched his head gingerly. "I'll do, I guess."

"I surely hope so!" She added, "I have to go, or I'll be late for work. I don't think I told you. I've got a job now— at Wright's store. Would you believe that Mister Murtaugh helped me to get it?"

Channing managed a smile. "I guess that fellow was good for something! Congratulations."

Emily was reluctant to leave. There were many questions she would have asked if she thought he would answer. He was so obstinate and so grudging of information about himself that she wondered why she should really care. Yet care she did, partly because the unknown quantity that was Burl Channing was involved with her growing confusions and doubts about Frank Killian. Nor would she soon forget the previous evening when this man had been so vulnerable and dependent on her help. There was something that wouldn't let a woman ever feel quite the same again about a man once he had been put in a position of needing her.

She excused herself with a final "Be careful—don't overdo. Perhaps you'd better let Doctor Clevenger have another look at you."

"We'll see," Channing said. He thanked her again, and she left.

The first point Bob Wright wanted to be made clear as she began her first day of work was that under no circumstances was she ever to wait on a male customer— he said it would scandalize the town and lose him business. With that stipulated and agreed to, he then put her to work familiarizing herself with the stock, the prices, and the general layout of store and stockroom. Later, he said, she could see if there was something she could help with in the office.

Emily knew from experience the hostility that could meet a woman trying to enter almost any line of work that was traditionally male. She had faced and overcome it at Jared McAfee's Mercantile in North Platte; she hoped to do the same here. For now, she would try to remain inconspicuous but still make herself useful, tidying displays and memorizing the layout of the store. A noisy bunch of Texas hands from one of the trail camps, with payoff money in their jeans, came trooping in, bent on acquiring complete new outfits. She got some curious stares but made it a point to stay well out of the way.

Then, toward midmorning, a woman entered the store, and Emily went gratefully to wait on her.

At a glance, she saw this was clearly no Dodge City housewife. She was too well dressed, too made up, her jet-black hair too artfully arranged. The woman asked to look at some yard goods. Emily very much doubted they had anything in stock flashy enough to suit her, but she led her to the proper counter. The woman looked over the bolts of cloth with a disdainful expression and fingered a sample or two. Suddenly, with an impatient shake of the head, she said quietly, "We're wasting time. I'm not really interested in this. I just wanted to have a look at you—maybe get a few words in." She added a quick warning. "But keep acting as though we're in business. I think your boss has his eye on you!"

Sure enough, when she looked around, Emily found Bob Wright's stare pinned on her. She quickly laid aside a bolt of goods and pulled forward another one. She said, "I don't understand. If you didn't come to buy anything—"

"You're Emily Barker," the woman hissed. "And I'm Cora."

"Who?"

"Cora Tyler." But when she'd said it, her expression altered a trifle; the antagonism that had been there seemed to lessen. "I guess you really haven't heard of me, have you? I sing over at the Comique." Her rouged lips quirked. "But then I guess he wouldn't tell you much about me—that wouldn't make sense."

"Just who is it you're talking about?" Emily demanded but with the disturbing conviction that she already knew.

"Do I have to spell it out for you? I mean Frank Killian. Who else?" When Emily only looked at her, the woman added sharply, "You think I'm stringing you! You don't think I even know him."

As she tried to collect her thoughts, Emily busied herself rewinding a bolt of goods. "He's never mentioned you," she asserted. "But it does sound as though he must have mentioned *me* to you!"

"Oh, yes, he's mentioned you plenty—until I'm sick

of it!" The woman shrugged. Her tone became bitter. "I can understand, though, you not wanting to believe any of this. There's something about us women: a man like Frank can tell us black's white, and like fools we'll swallow it!"

Emily said slowly, "I don't think you're lying when you claim to know Frank Killian—"

"I not only claim it; if you'll let me, I can show the proof—I mean now! Otherwise, I guess we got nothing more to say to each other. . . . When I heard you was working here, I decided I had to have a look at you for myself." And Cora Tyler gave her rival a bold, slow stare that took her in from head to toe. After that, she stepped back with a gesture that dismissed the counter and its display of cloth. Loudly enough to carry if Wright or someone else was listening, she said, "No, I just can't use any of this. Thanks all the same for your trouble." She turned to leave.

Emily made a decision. "Wait outside for me," she said swiftly. She proceeded to straighten up the counter as Cora Tyler walked out of the store. Afterward, she went looking for Bob Wright and caught up with him as he was about to enter his office. "Mister Wright," she said in apology, "I hate to ask my first day, but something really important has come up. Could I take an hour? I'll make up for it."

He looked sour, but she must have convinced him of her sincerity. He nodded curtly, first checking the time on the silver watch he took from his vest pocket. "An hour," he said. Emily grabbed her hat and coat and hurried out to where Cora Tyler waited.

Chapter 11

Burl Channing decided against seeing the doctor. He was greatly improved, and a slight tendency to double vision had cleared itself up overnight. Now he felt rested and clear-headed, with only a trace of dull headache remaining to bother him. By the time he had brushed the dried mud from his clothing, dressed, and shaved—moving carefully, not rushing himself—he was convinced any damage he took the previous night had not been permanent.

What did bother him was the thought of blacking out and being thrown, helpless, on the charity of Emily Barker, a woman who apparently disliked him. It was irritating to be so unsure of what went on after he made his way up the steps to his room. Vaguely, he remembered someone who must have been the doctor, but—who else? *Had* there been a second man in the room with them? Emily hadn't mentioned him, but why should there be this strong, though muddled, impression of another presence and a voice he hadn't recognized?

It had been one of the hotel's other guests, he supposed, and nothing to bother about. But it did bother him not to know.

For breakfast, he relied heavily on several cups of strong black coffee. Afterward, he went out onto the porch of the Dodge House, chose a barrel chair that looked comfortable, and fired up a cheroot he had bought at the desk in the lobby. He settled himself to see what happened next.

The broken cloud cover and showery weather of the last few days had ended, and this morning the sun stood in a clear sky, shining warmly and picking glints of dazzle from puddles in the rutted length of Front Street; before long, the puddles would shrink and the mud would begin to dry up and crack and turn into the familiar dust of a plains summer. There seemed to be more of the Texas cattle crews in town since yesterday. Their numbers would continue to increase as the weeks passed and Dodge took on the character of a prosperous shipping town approaching the height of the season.

Channing sat at ease, enjoying his smoke and watching a flow of traffic—and knowing that he, in turn, was being watched. He ignored the covert stares he received. He was not only taking it easy after his ordeal of the night before, but he had a strategy, and he was acting on it. He'd laid the groundwork, and now he had only to sit here, patient and untroubled, doing nothing at all, in order to apply the pressure to Frank Killian and achieve what he was after.

So he was not surprised when, at last, a man approached and halted on the sidewalk near him. It was the swamper from the Long Branch, and that indicated things were about to pay off; but Channing gave no sign of anxiousness; he simply nodded good morning. The man handed over a folded piece of paper, saying, "I was paid to bring you this."

Channing flipped a coin over the railing for him to catch— "A little something more for your trouble." As

126

the swamper shuffled off down the street, Burl Channing took his deliberate time about opening the paper.

There was a single sentence: "I'm at the Long Branch." It had no signature. It didn't need one.

So he finally had what he wanted; but, with curious eyes on him, he wasn't going to show too strong a reaction. He didn't want a crowd where he was going. He refolded the note and pocketed it and continued to enjoy his cigar as though he had nothing more urgent in mind. Presently, he eased to his feet, gave his gun belt a hitch, then came down off the hotel porch and started west toward the Long Branch, not hurrying.

A familiar figure stood near the door of the saloon, watching him approach. As he came up, Wes Lowe nodded a curt greeting, the eyes in the gunman's narrow face sharply observant. He said, "How do you feel?"

Channing said, "All right."

"Last night, I wasn't so sure. You were looking pretty glassy eyed when I dropped you off at the hotel. I thought you might need a doctor."

Channing, who saw no point in telling him everything, simply shrugged. But when he started to pass, Lowe made a gesture to detain him. "Your man's in there," he said, and added, "I'm going in with you."

"No."

"I think I'd better. You still don't look too good. And he's brought some help with him."

Channing registered that news. He wasn't eager for interference from Wes Lowe no matter what odds Killian might have in his favor. Still he suspected there was no good way to keep this man from doing whatever he felt like. Channing said gruffly, "Suit yourself. But I want you to stay clear."

He walked inside, the gunman following.

For so early in the day, the place held something of a crowd. Men lined the bar and the sides of the room, and Chalk Beeson himself had joined his bartender behind the long counter. Even so, no one seemed to be doing much; whatever activity there was ceased the moment Channing entered. He felt the weight of their quiet stares, but he had been expecting this. He gave the crowd no more than a glance. Instead, he looked the length of the narrow, windowless room to the tables at the far end. He didn't have to be told that the man seated there alone was Frank Killian.

Apparently, Killian's faro game was open for business. The hinged, baize-covered faro layout, with its replica of the twelve cards of the deck waiting to be covered by bets, lay open in front of him along with chips and coppers, the case keeper—a contraption resembling an abacus—and the dealing box. The lean fingers of Killian's left hand toyed with a stack of chips as he faced the door. The skylight above his head poured down the only brightness in the shadowed barroom. The brim of Killian's derby shielded his eyes and cast his face into darkness; but Channing, advancing down the center of the room between a double line of spectators, had sufficient view of the gambler's spare features, the good cut of his coat, the linen shirt and black string tie. His right hand was out of sight below the top of the table.

And then Channing came abruptly to a halt. His eyes shifted to the man who stood beside Killian's chair, shoulders leaning comfortably against the wall, the smoke from his cigarette twisting blue-gray toward the skylight. He looked like any trail hand. But it was sight of the eyebrows—like a single black bar across the bridge of the man's nose—and the purple bruise staining one broad cheekbone that shortened the breath in Channing's throat and made the sore knuckles of his right hand suddenly begin to ache again.

Frank Killian's smooth voice brought Channing's glance back. In an expressionless tone, Killian said, "You're Channing, I take it. I understand you've been asking for me. Somehow we keep missing connections. What's on your mind? If you're looking for a chance to buck my game, all you have to do is take a seat."

He sounded calm and self-confident enough, but Channing had a feeling the man was holding himself carefully in check. Perhaps it was more than the hot light pouring down on him that put a sheen of moisture around his mouth. Killian must have nerved himself up to come out and meet this challenge in public.

Channing said, "I'm not interested in your game, Killian."

"Something else, then? Maybe we should have a drink and then find a place alone where we can discuss it."

"Later. Right now I want both your hands on the table—where I can see them."

That slipped past the other man's guard. Killian's shoulders stiffened. Nevertheless, he brought the right hand up from his lap and into view; the hand was empty. He said, "I don't know just what you—"

Channing cut him off, indicating the man who stood against the wall. "Is this a friend of yours?"

"Jim Fitch?" Killian answered carefully. "We've done some business."

"He does his business in dark alleys!" Channing said coolly. Suddenly, he was moving forward, narrowing the distance at a stride. "The next time you come after me, cowpoke," he told Fitch through lips gone tight with quick fury, "you'd better finish the job, or you'll get worse than a black eye!"

The man's stare flickered, and as Channing closed on him, he became rattled; he started a hand toward the front of his jacket. Channing savagely knocked the hand aside and instantly snatched the six-shooter from behind the man's waist belt. He held it up, and Jim Fitch went motionless. "Is this the one that got laid across my skull last night?" he demanded. "How much were you paid to do that job?"

When the man's mouth worked soundlessly, Channing ordered him, "Speak up! Or would you rather see for yourself how it feels?" Deliberately, he used the gun's muzzle to poke the shapeless hat from the man's head and pressed the barrel alongside his skull. Anger made Channing's hand shake.

Jim Fitch was sweating, his face contorted as he tried to cringe away from the touch of the gun barrel. Suddenly, he broke, crying out in pure terror, "Frank! He means it! If you don't want me talking, for God's sake, do something—I ain't going to stand here and have my head bashed in!"

Frank Killian was jarred into motion. The legs of his chair screeched, and he was on his feet, a short-barreled pistol sliding into sight from under his coat. Burl Channing spun to face this danger when the harsh voice of Chalk Beeson sounded suddenly through the room: "First one uses a gun—I'll drop him!"

Everything stopped. Channing and Killian turned to see the owner of the Long Branch with both elbows planted on the bar, his hands holding a six-shooter at eye level, trained at them. Beside him, the bartender was just hauling a sawed-off shotgun from under the counter.

Burl Channing lowered the weapon he was holding; Killian let his own slide back into its shoulder holster. At that, an audible sigh went through the room. Unnoticed by anyone but Channing, Wes Lowe quietly lowered the hand he'd lifted toward the gap in his own coat front.

"There's never been any violence in the Long Branch," the saloon owner said, "and I ain't letting anybody spoil my record for me. You'll oblige me by putting that down," he added, indicating the gun Channing had taken from Jim Fitch; Channing laid it on the table.

Wes Lowe spoke up. "Friend, if you'd been waylaid and pistol whipped by Killian's thugs—"

"Chalk, it's a lie!" Killian had found his tongue. "The whole thing's a lie! Not me or Jim Fitch knows about it!"

Somebody said, "What the hell! We just now heard him admit it."

"A man will admit anything with a gun at his head!"

Chalk Beeson overrode Killian. "What do *you* say, Channing. I hear you're a federal marshal—that's the reason you're allowed to wear a gun against the ordinance. Just how far do you intend to push this?"

"As far as I have to," Burl Channing replied flatly. He indicated Killian. "I came to Dodge City looking for this man in connection with a murder last summer in Nebraska. Now I've caught up with him."

"You carry a warrant?" the saloon man suggested. "Extradition papers and the like?"

Channing had to repeat what he had told Ed Masterson. "I'm not wearing my badge. But the dead man was a friend of mine."

"I see." Beeson's scowl deepened. "A private war, in other words. Well, I won't allow anything like that in my place of business! Take it somewhere else to settle it."

Chalk Beeson appeared to be adamant, and he had the whip hand. Burl Channing gritted his teeth. He was beginning to see the situation he had let himself be maneuvered into. It only added to his anger to look at Killian and see the beginning of triumph on the gambler's face.

But that faded instantly at what Beeson had to say next: "As for you, Killian—from this minute you're through working the Long Branch. The sooner you leave, the better."

The man's head snapped. Words stumbled from lips gone slack. "What! Hell, Chalk! You can't mean this!"

"I mean it! I haven't much liked the way you've been running your game; now I've got a good excuse to get you out of here. Luke Shantz, for one, has been offering to come in with me and handle the gambling concession, and I think I'll take him up on it.

"As for what happened in Nebraska, I don't pretend to know the straight of that or care much. But you were willing to invite your personal enemy into the Long Branch for a showdown with scum like this to back you up." A contemptuous jerk of the head indicated Jim Fitch. "That I won't put up with!"

Under this tirade, Frank Killian's face had lost color, and his expression had gone from one of disbelief to fury. Channing was near enough to see the glitter of his eyes, the leap of a muscle in one lean cheek. Beeson didn't wait for an argument. "I can hold on to your layout for you till you let me know where you want it sent. Just now I think it would be a good idea if you take your alley rat with you and leave before I'm tempted to have you both run in for carrying concealed weapons north of the deadline. Or I might even turn you over to the marshal here!"

Someone in the room let out a snicker, whether of amusement or only in release of tension; in any event, Frank Killian turned brick red. He looked around him. The street door, at the far end of the long room, must have seemed too great a distance to run the gauntlet of staring eyes and grinning faces. Instead, he gave Jim Fitch a glance and a summoning nod of the head. Fitch paused only long enough to snatch up his pistol; after that, he went sidling along the wall to a back door, which he opened. Killian was close behind him, his attention still fastened on Channing. In the doorway, he paused to throw a warning at his pursuer. "Don't come after me!"

Next moment, he was gone, and the door slammed shut.

Channing actually took a step to follow, but a word from Chalk Beeson checked him: "Marshal!" Turning, he saw the saloon owner shake his head; the gun was held loosely, not pointing at him but still a threat. At the moment, there was nothing to do but let Frank Killian go. Channing settled his shoulders, trying not to show his baffled anger.

In what sounded like an attempt at conciliation, Beeson now suggested, "Have a drink on the house, Channing."

"I guess not."

"You're sore because I wouldn't let you have him," Beeson said. "After all, the man did work here; I owed him that much. But no more. I don't want anything further to do with him."

Channing shrugged, his temper now coming under better control. "I'm not sore at you," he said gruffly. "But that's a second time he's got away from me. Now I start all over again." He turned and walked out the front door, leaving a buzz of excited talk swelling behind him.

On the street, the dazzle of sunlight was punishing to the eyes after the dimness of the saloon's interior. His head was aching again dully. Finding Wes Lowe still at his elbow, he said angrily, "He slipped through my hands again! I finally brought him out into the open, and then I lost him—my own fault for losing my temper."

"How about trying the alley?"

"No use. Beeson gave him time enough; he'll be gone by now."

"So what do we do next?"

Channing looked at the other man. "We?"

"You refused my help before," Wes Lowe said, "but I'm beginning to think you need it. I'd be obliged to take a hand."

"Not even asking more about what this manhunt is all about?"

"A murder, you said." The gunman shrugged. "I imagined you had reasons for what you're doing. Anyhow, I'm beginning to think I don't much like this fellow Killian. I know I don't like the way he operates!"

"He's a slippery one," Channing agreed. "To avoid facing me, he tried to have me waylaid and killed. When that didn't work, he had to come out in the open, but he was careful to have his man Fitch on hand to tilt the odds."

"And instead," the gunman finished, "he got himself laughed at and kicked out of the Long Branch. It must have been as humiliating a thing as ever happened to him. By now, he should be desperate. He might sneak out of Dodge, but the story would only follow him. It's my guess he'll head for cover while he licks his wounds and decides what to do next."

"My guess, too." Channing nodded. "It looks as

though I'm going to have to go in and dig him out of his hole."

They looked across the sun-soaked expanse of Front Street and the Plaza. Wes Lowe asked, "Do we have any idea at all where that hole would be?"

"An idea—nothing more," Channing said. "One I haven't wanted to act on, but now I suppose I shouldn't have waited this long. By my reckoning, the trail starts yonder at that place they call the Comique. . . ."

Chapter 12

Though Emily had been brave enough to risk the dangers of Front Street alone, to venture south of the Plaza—even in the full light of midday—was something she would never have had the courage to do; but now she had the company of Cora Tyler, who, after all, belonged to this rough world below the deadline and knew every foot of it. Emily could only try to guess where she was being taken. Her companion wasted no words. She could only keep pace with Cora's determined stride and wait and see.

They came to an alley of unpainted shacks, and Cora Tyler turned in at one of these. The door was unlocked. She simply threw it open and ushered her guest inside. There appeared to be only two rooms to the place. The first, comprised of living and eating quarters, had a couple of battered wing chairs and a sofa; also, a kitchen table with an oilcloth cover, a cookstove, a sink, and a pump.

"It don't amount to much," the woman said roughly as she watched Emily look about her, "but it has a roof." The walls were cheaply papered; there were curtains at the windows, worn linoleum underfoot, and a couple of gaudy magazine covers nailed up for decoration.

Without waiting for a comment, Cora crossed and opened another door, motioning Emily to follow her. Here was the sleeping room, filled by a large double bed and dresser; a closet in one corner was screened by a curtain. The bed was rumpled and unmade. As Emily hesitated in the doorway, Cora made an attempt to straighten the bed clothes but quickly gave it up with a shrug, admitting, "All right. So I'm a sloppy housekeeper! Just look around you," she said. "And then look at this . . ." She stepped to the closet and swept the curtain aside. After that, she stood by to watch Emily's face.

Cora Tyler's wardrobe, even including the dresses she wore at the Comique, was fairly limited. But the closet contained other things—a man's clothing and a suit just like the one Frank Killian had been wearing the evening Emily first met him. A man's button shoes were on the closet floor beside a pair of patent leather pumps that belonged to the woman. Emily felt herself go numb as she turned her attention to the dresser top.

Besides a pitcher and washbowl, it contained an untidy collection of toilet articles—jars and bottles, a curling iron and china hair receiver, but also a shaving mug and a pair of silver military brushes. She picked one up and saw the florid letters "F.K." etched on its back. She recognized the amethyst stickpin Frank Killian had worn in his cravat the day she met him. And amidst the clutter there was a photograph in a wooden frame: Frank seated stiffly against a studio backdrop and Cora Tyler standing beside him with her hand on his shoulder.

The woman saw Emily looking at it and said, "That picture was taken in Kansas City just last month, when we were on a little trip to see the sights. . . ."

Emily looked at her. "I don't know what you're

trying to prove," she said coldly. "I certainly never imagined that I was the first woman Frank Killian had ever been interested in. He said as much himself."

"And I suppose he said, now he'd found *you,* that other stuff was all behind him! Well, does this look like it's behind him?" Cora indicated the room with the wave of a hand. She sounded quite in earnest as she continued. "Honey, I ain't trying to hurt you. I just think you ought to know the truth. It's no unusual thing for Frank Killian to suddenly find him a new woman and throw her in my face, just like he did with you. Hell! You make the third in the six months since he came to Dodge!

"You're his luck—is that what he told you? I thought so," she said, seeing her answer in Emily's face. "It's what he told *me* once. He's such a jumble of gambler's superstitions, he may even believe it for a while. But *love*? Honey, a man like that ain't able to love anyone but himself! All he knows is how to use people. Like he's used me all along. Like he's been using *you* to help him keep tabs on what that fellow Channing was up to!

"Oh, yes! Didn't you realize that?" She added bitterly, "And right now, when he needs a place to hide— well, you can see who it is he's run to! I suggest you do some thinking while you still have time!" And with that she walked out of the room, leaving Emily with the things she had been hearing.

They had the ring of truth. She couldn't escape the fact that after that moment in her hotel room last night, with protestations of love still on his lips, Frank Killian had left her and returned here to this house. He'd discussed her with Cora Tyler—had passed along the news that she would be starting work today at Wright & Beverley's—and then he had slept with the woman in this very bed. . . .

Emily shook her head, unable to reconcile her feelings and her doubts.

Then she heard the outer door open and close again; someone was talking to Cora in the other room. She caught an exclamation from Cora Tyler and an indistinguishable answer in a voice she recognized as Frank Killian's. She moved into the doorway and stood staring.

Killian had lost his hat somewhere; his string tie was undone, his hair plastered to his forehead with perspiration, his face ashen. He stood with his shoulders pressed against the outside door, and his ragged breathing seemed to fill the room. Emily heard Cora exclaim, "Frank! What is it now? What's happened?"

"Everything's gone to hell!" he told her hoarsely. "That Channing. Damn him, I'll—!" His words broke off as he caught sight of Emily in the bedroom doorway. He stiffened. "What are *you* doing here?"

He pushed away from the door and came toward her. Stunned, Emily tried to speak and couldn't, but he must have read something in her face that warned him of a change in her. Suddenly, he halted and whirled on the other woman, and there was madness in him. "You slut! This is your doing! Don't deny it. You deliberately brought her here, trying to turn her against me. . . ." His hand whipped around and struck Cora. The woman's head was thrown to the side, hard.

But she recovered instantly and in the next moment was coming at him, silent as a tigress, the nails of one hand raking down his cheek. Killian swore and flung her off and then went after her. His open hand struck back and forth, first one side of her face and then the other as, cursing, he drove her backward. Her dark hair came down from its pins. Blood sprang from a mashed lip.

By that time, Emily had broken free of the first

shock; she got to them and grabbed at the man's arm, crying, "Frank! Stop this!" The face he turned to her was like nothing she had ever seen—the mark of Cora's nails across it, the eyes blazing, the mouth twisted in ugly fury. Emily drew back from him.

Cora had been sent stumbling against the edge of the sink; now, as Killian moved toward her again, he stopped suddenly. Light glinted from the blade of a butcher knife in her grasp. Her eyes were wild, her black hair flying, as she said through bleeding lips, "All right, you sonofabitch! You just try and lay another finger on me!"

Killian halted, warily eying the point of the knife leveled at him and the woman crouched tensely behind it. He started a movement toward the gap of his coat, held it as she warned, "Go ahead—I wouldn't put it past you to use that gun. Try! You'll be dead before you reach it!"

This time, it was Frank Killian who retreated a step and then another. As he fell back, Cora advanced, knife point threatening, her stare pinned to his face. Emily thought she heard a strain of terror in his voice as he cried, "Don't be a fool, Cora!"

Cora Tyler touched her fingers to her mouth, looked at the blood on them, and said, "By rights I ought to thank you—for helping me realize how often I *have* been a fool for you! Well, it won't happen again. I swear it won't!" She threw a bitter look at Emily. "Maybe you still want him? Feel welcome—I'll never fight you for the privilege!"

That brought Killian's attention back to Emily. When he saw she was going to say nothing, he cried hoarsely, "Emily, I don't know what she's said—what she's done to poison your mind against me. But don't turn against me now. You've got to give me a hearing. . . ."

But all Emily could feel, looking at his sweating face

with the scoring of Cora's nails down his cheek, was deep revulsion. The face he had just shown her was one she would never be able to forget. It was as though she had now truly seen him for the first time. Slowly, she shook her head. "I think you and I both have made a mistake, Frank."

"No! Listen to me!" he insisted, and despite the threat of Cora's knife blade, he took a step toward Emily. But she turned her back, shutting him out.

Behind her, she heard Cora Tyler tell the man, "Why don't you just leave?" For a moment, there was no answer except for his harsh breathing. Abruptly, Killian's heavy footsteps crossed the linoleum; there was the sound of the door being wrenched open and slammed shut.

Emily came about in time to see Cora fling the butcher knife hard at the wooden panel. It sank deep and stood quivering while she dropped her face into her hands and began to sob. She sat down heavily at the table.

Emily went to her. She asked with real concern, "Did he hurt you badly?" The woman shook her head, hair tumbling in disarray about her. Emily tried again: "Perhaps I could have a look—"

"No—I'm all right." Cora dug a handkerchief out of her dress pocket and dabbed it at the hurt lip; the bleeding appeared to have stopped. She dried her eyes. She was trembling, whether from grief or anger or merely in reaction to the violence. In a tone of infinite bitterness, she added, "I can't think why the hell it should matter to you!"

"You did nothing to me," Emily insisted quietly. "As a matter of fact, I should be grateful."

"Maybe we both should," Cora Tyler admitted.

"I could use a drink," she said a few minutes later, getting up from the table where the two of them had sat talking. "How about yourself?" When Emily shook her head, the other woman said, "Well, I hope you'll excuse me while I do!" She opened a cupboard and got out a bottle and a glass and poured whiskey. Seated again, she drained it off and swore a little as it stung her hurt lip.

She toyed with the glass, then said with a frown, "I still wonder what's been going on that he didn't want to tell me about. Early last evening, he seemed to think he had taken care of this federal marshal that was after him; but something must have gone wrong because later he said it looked like he would have to meet him today, after all. Well, I suppose we'll be hearing about it."

Mention of Burl Channing had given Emily a stab of guilty conscience, remembering how she had deceived him from the first and concealed the fact she had been seeing Frank Killian while she knew of the lawman's efforts to find him. She was moved now to ask, "Did he tell you anything about what took place in Nebraska before he came to Dodge? About someone being killed there?"

"Honey," the woman said, "he never so much as mentioned Nebraska. He never told me nothing about himself—and I had sense enough to know it was no use asking. He was one close-mouthed bastard when he wanted to be."

After a moment, Emily said, "It's time I was getting back to my job. I promised I wouldn't be gone more than an hour."

"You'll still be staying in Dodge, then?"

"For now. I've got a lot of thinking to get through."

With sudden resolution, Cora Tyler slapped her empty tumbler on the table. "I know what *I'm* going to do!" she said, and leaped to her feet.

"What?"

142

Curious, Emily rose and followed her as far as the bedroom door. Cora was at the closet, furiously ripping Killian's garments off their hooks and flinging them onto the floor in a heap. "I'm burning them!" she declared loudly. "That'll teach him!" She went to the dresser and proceeded to sweep aside his other possessions. "All this stuff! I'll clean it out, and then there'll be nothing for the sonofabitch to come back for!" The photograph from Kansas City joined the rest in a tinkle of broken glass.

And then Cora caught a glimpse of herself in the dresser mirror and must have realized the state of her appearance. She swore again and got to work setting things straight, pulling pins and trying to put her dark hair into some semblance of order while Emily watched dumbly, not knowing what to say. It was then that a knock sounded at the street door. "That better not be him!" Cora exclaimed under her breath, and swept past Emily to the door. With her hand on the knob, she demanded, "Who's there?"

The answer, through the knife-gouged panel, was indistinct. After a moment's indecision, the woman pulled it open. "Well?"

A voice Emily knew well said, "Miss Tyler, I haven't wanted to drag you into this. But if Frank Killian is here, I mean to have him!"

"Oh, you do?" She stepped back, throwing the door wide. "Marshal, any part of that bastard you can find here you're welcome to! You gents step in."

Burl Channing entered with Wes Lowe behind him. When he saw Emily, astonishment and incredulity showed on the marshal's face.

What followed was, for Emily, the most excruciatingly difficult time of all. There was nothing for it now but to make a full and clean explanation so Channing could understand how he happened to find her here with Cora Tyler and what her role had been in shaping the events that led to this moment. She told it as they sat at Cora's table—all except Wes Lowe, who stayed on his feet as he listened and silently prowled the room with the restlessness of a dangerous animal.

Emily held back nothing of her story, beginning with the letter from Jared McAfee and the terms on which she had agreed to deliver it. As she told of how she deliberately eluded Channing on their arrival here in Dodge City so she could reach Killian ahead of him, she saw the marshal's face go bleak, the muscles of his jaws set hard. To see her actions through his eyes made her confession all the more difficult. But at the moment she was glad to end the deception.

Finally, he put a question: "This letter you brought mentioned me by name? It said I was on my way to kill him?"

"Apparently, that's what Mister McAfee believed. He told me he had an obligation to Frank Killian—that's why he felt he had to warn him."

The man's eyes seemed to bore into her as he said, "From the start, it's baffled me how the fellow could have been waiting and ready the night I arrived and all set to try an ambush. Now at least I know."

"Now you know," Emily agreed miserably. "If he had killed you, it would have been my fault!"

"Tell me this: last night, when you had to help me into my room—was *he* there?"

"Yes. He had come up for a talk. I sent him out to fetch the doctor."

"I just wondered. This morning at the Long Branch, when I saw Killian for the very first time, I had the oddest

144

flash of memory—the two of you together, holding a lamp and looking down at me. But of course I couldn't believe that because you'd never once hinted that you knew him. And of course I never doubted you."

Emily looked at her hands, knotted tightly together where they lay on the table in front of her. "I'm sorry. Please believe me!" To her, the words sounded inadequate and lame. How could she explain her attraction to Killian, stemming from his superficial resemblance to her dead husband? Even worse, how could she expect a man she'd misjudged the way she had Burl Channing to trust her again after her lies and betrayals?

Cora, who had been listening to all this, asked Channing, "Just why do you want Frank Killian, anyway—if you're *not* gunning for him? It's my opinion you've done a pretty good job yourself keeping everybody in the dark; in which case, some of the blame for all this is rightly yours."

"That could be," he conceded gruffly. "I've always kept my affairs to myself. Maybe that isn't always a good idea. . . . Well, let me ask you both something: Has Killian ever mentioned, to either of you, the name of Tom Nolan?"

The women exchanged a look. "That's a new one on me," Cora Tyler said.

Emily asked, "Who is Tom Nolan?"

"He was my friend," Channing answered. "As fine a man as I ever knew. Last summer, up in North Platte, he was murdered and robbed of twenty-five thousand dollars. That same evening, a down-at-the-heels gambler named Frank Killian had met him and stuck to him like a leech; he was the last man to be seen with Tom. Next morning, when Nolan's body was found, Killian was gone, and so was the money. There was no further trace of him until about a week ago when I learned he'd been seen here in Dodge doing great business over a faro layout."

Emily said slowly, remembering, "He did tell me his trouble with you had something to do with a killing—that he wasn't guilty, though you thought he was."

"All I ever wanted was to find out the truth; take him back to North Platte if necessary for an investigation. If he can prove he's innocent, then he'll have no more trouble with me. But he doesn't act like someone who's innocent!"

"He had plenty of money on him when he hit Dodge early last fall sometime," Cora volunteered. "He told me he'd got it all gambling."

"I don't see how. In North Platte, he couldn't even buy his own drinks! It makes me wonder what obligation a businessman like Jared McAfee could possibly owe to a tinhorn gambler; but that's McAfee's problem. *My* problem"—Channing got to his feet—"is that I've just missed one more chance at Killian!

"But at least we've cleared the air, Miss Tyler, and I'm glad of that. The question is, what next? Up to now, Killian's been going on arrogance and his faith in his own luck. He thought he could hide out here while the killers he'd hired took care of me. That didn't quite work. And today he was closed out of the Long Branch, and now that you've kicked him out, what is there left for him in Dodge City? Has the time come for him to sneak away like he did from North Platte? Or, if he stays, where do I look for him next?"

"I'll have to think about that one," Cora said, frowning. "There's one thing I can tell you: Frank owns a horse—a chestnut gelding that he won in a high-stakes game last winter. He keeps it at Bell's livery. He's crazy about that horse; he'd never leave without it."

Burl Channing glanced quickly in Wes Lowe's direction. The man needed no instructions; he nodded and without a word slipped silently from the room— going to check at Bell's, of course. Channing turned back to the women.

He said, "Frank Killian is a hard man to come to grips with. Maybe he thinks I'll give up and quit—but I don't quit that easy. Sooner or later, I'm going to back him into a hole he can't get out of—however long it takes me. That's a promise I've made to Tom Nolan and Tom's widow. And to myself. . . ."

Chapter 13

As it turned out, that was not going to be an easy promise to keep. In the next few days, it began to look as though the ground had opened up and swallowed Frank Killian.

For Burl Channing they were days of growing frustration. He would not have believed it possible that a man could go underground and not leave some trace in a place as small as Dodge City. He spent long hours haunting Front Street and the South Side, making the rounds of saloons and dives. He rubbed elbows with gamblers and with soldiers from the fort, with hide hunters and freighters, and, in growing numbers, with cowhands from the Texas herds that were trailing in to fill up the holding grounds around Dodge. He asked questions, and he watched and listened, and he learned nothing whatever.

In frequenting the rough district below the deadline, he knew very well he was in danger. Already, except for the intervention of Ed Masterson, he had nearly been killed there. Killian's friends might be waiting for a second chance. But though he walked carefully and kept his hand near his gun, there was never a threat or hint of attack. Jim Fitch, too, seemed to have vanished completely.

Killian's horse—the chestnut—was in its stall at the livery. Ham Bell promised to send word should anyone try to claim it. The days passed; word never came. Meanwhile, Channing kept an eye on the stage line's schedule, and each day at train time he was at the depot, making sure his man didn't try to escape by that route. But there was never any sign of Frank Killian.

One noon, Jack Murtaugh hailed Channing on the depot platform, a sample case in each hand and his railroad ticket between his teeth. Murtaugh set down his cases, removed the ticket, and pumped the marshal's hand as he wished him a hearty farewell.

"I'm off for Denver," he said in his usual boisterous good humor. "The old mile-high city—some promising new accounts to look up there. Maybe our paths will cross again. Meanwhile, you'll give my best regards to Mrs. Barker, won't you?" Channing promised and at the conductor's call watched the fat man go scrambling aboard the cars, coattails flying, just in time before the train pulled away.

Sometimes, he thought, he could almost envy a man like that—thick-skinned and uncomplicated, with nothing more to worry him than the next meal, the next contact, the next sale.

Besides the missing gambler, Channing had Emily Barker on his mind. From time to time, he ran into her in the hallway or dining room of the Dodge House or going to or from her job. They were always polite, but a coolness separated them. Something in the way Emily looked at him disturbed Channing very much. He understood now, as he could not have before, the way in which Frank Killian had stood between them; but now that Killian was no longer in the picture, Channing would have liked to try

149

making friends with Emily Barker. But something held him back. She had made it all too clear, all too often, that she disapproved of him.

He threw himself with single-minded purpose into the manhunt. He had begun to feel like a cat that watches a deserted rat hole, but he wasn't ready even to consider giving up. Wes Lowe, who seemed to be spending most of his time playing stud poker in one or another of Dodge City's saloons and card houses, twice passed on a rumor that Frank Killian was still in Dodge. Channing doggedly checked out every clue and every lead, but nothing came of it. He followed his routine and wrote to Maude Nolan, informing her of his lack of success.

And he waited.

On the evening of the fourth day, Wes Lowe invited Channing into the Alhambra to offer a drink and a suggestion. The April weather had turned mild after two days of wet and blustery chill. Now, with the arrival of three big herds in as many days, Dodge City was suddenly buzzing with activity. The streets rang to the chime of spurs and the twangy sound of raucous Texas voices. Over the wide flats of the Arkansas River, the glow of cook fires marked the trail camps where thousands of longhorned cattle were being loose held. At the stock pens, on the railroad spur, sweating men worked by lantern light to finish shoving the last of a cattle shipment up the ramps and into waiting cars.

"Town's growing lively," Channing commented. "It'll be more or less like this clear up to October."

Wes Lowe said, "No sign of Killian. You think he's in Dodge?"

"I have to think so."

The gunman made circles on the bar top with the bottom of his glass. "I've got a notion," he said. "With a town full of drovers and well-heeled buyers, there must be some big money floating around. A man like Killian should be in his element—only, just now, his faro layout is still locked up at the Long Branch, and he's not getting any of it. That is, unless—"

"Unless what?" Channing prompted as the man paused to finish his drink.

"The fellow's a gambler—a pro. Without his layout, he can't function. Besides, he can't lie low forever without going broke. On the other hand, the kind of money I'm talking about isn't apt to be found floating around the bars. The high-stakes action tends to happen in private card rooms—tucked away in places you least expect. Flush out those games and there's a chance you'll find your man."

Channing nodded. "It's a good notion, maybe not too easy to act on."

"Not impossible. I keep my ears open; I sometimes hear things."

"Fair enough. But if you turn anything up, check with me before you make a move. Trying to crash a high-stakes game where outsiders aren't welcome could be risky. Don't take chances."

"I never take chances," Wes Lowe said as he turned to leave. "And I don't work miracles. But I thought the idea was worth mentioning."

Sometime later, as he stood on the sidewalk and looked across the darkened Plaza to the noisy hubbub and the lights of the South Side, Channing asked himself for the hundredth time where, in this small area of a few square blocks, Killian could be hiding. How much longer could this unprofitable search go on? A light rig with a weary-looking horse between the shafts drew up beside him. Its occupant leaned out, and there was enough spill of light from a nearby saloon window for him to recognize the sheriff. "Channing?"

He nodded to Bat Masterson. "Thought it was you standing there," the sheriff said. Masterson took off his derby, wiped grime and sweat from his face, and then ran the handkerchief around the sweatband of his hat. "Been out in the county for a few days. Didn't hardly expect to find you still here. You still on the hunt? No sign of your man yet?"

"No sign," Channing admitted.

"After all this time, my guess would be he's left. He must have got by you."

"I don't think so."

Masterson shook his head. "My brother Ed has his men on the watch, too. If none of you can turn up anything pretty soon, you'd best chuck it in."

Burl Channing was not one to admit discouragement. "I'm a stubborn man, Bat."

Just then a spatter of gunfire sounded south of the Plaza—several rapid shots. Bat Masterson exclaimed, "Now what the devil? Sounded like a damned Gatling gun!"

Channing stepped off the sidewalk and into the street, trying to get a better look at the lights across the empty Plaza. There was no more shooting, but he could see people moving around and hear a babble of voices. Men were pouring out of one of the buildings. He said, "Looks to me like the Lady Gay. . . ."

Masterson confirmed it and added, "Sounds like the

152

trouble is over. Don't reckon there's any need for me to stick my nose in. That's Ed's department, and I don't like to interfere. He or one of his boys will get it under control."

They stayed where they were, watching and listening in silence. Over there, a couple of hundred yards across the weedy expanse of Plaza, the excitement continued. All at once, Channing said, "Somebody's coming."

A figure was making its way toward them across the Plaza. Dimly visible, it came on at what seemed an unhurried pace; presently, it was close enough so they could hear dry weeds crackling underfoot. Now they could make him out—a man, bareheaded, holding himself stiffly erect. Next moment, Bat Masterson swore and leaped down from the buggy's seat. He ran across Front Street, and Burl Channing was close behind him.

Ed Masterson stumbled into the glow of streaking lamplight. He looked at them. He said, in an odd voice, "I've been shot!" And he collapsed into his brother's arms—Bat was barely able to catch him and ease him to the ground.

Even in that poor light it was impossible to miss the ghastly wound in the middle of the man's body. Channing saw that Ed Masterson's clothes were smoldering. Somebody must have shoved the muzzle of a gun against his belly and let go. A shot can blow a man in two that way.

Bat Masterson, on his knees beside his brother, said tightly, "Channing. Find out who did it!"

The other hesitated. "You need help with him. We've got to get the doctor!"

"I'll have help," the sheriff said; indeed, men were coming out of the buildings along Front Street. The sheriff turned and yelled to them, and they came hurrying. Channing turned without a word and set off across the uneven ground of the Plaza.

At the Lady Gay, he found a crowd milling around the entrance to the dance hall—customers, mostly, mingling with a few girls who worked there. Channing pulled a bartender aside.

"It was one of those damn things!" The bartender shook his head sadly. "There was half dozen of them in here, drunk and cutting up pretty rough. Ed and his deputy, Nat Haywood, came in to quiet them down. I heard Ed order them to check their guns at the bar. But they never did, and when he left, a couple of them followed him out. I didn't see the rest of it, but I was told Ed tried to rassle the gun away from one, and the fellow rammed it into his guts and let him have it.

"Ed got his gun out and put a couple of slugs into both of them. And then damned if he didn't just turn and walk away before anyone had a chance to see if he was bad hurt."

"Where was the deputy?"

"I guess it all happened too fast for him. I understand the two that Masterson shot went running into Peacock's saloon, and Haywood went after them."

Channing hurriedly thanked the man. There were more people crowding in front of Peacock's. He pushed his way inside and found Deputy Haywood attempting to clear a space around two wounded men who had collapsed bloodily on the floor. Channing caught sight of someone he knew—Ham Bell, the liveryman. With a look of sour distaste, Bell told him, "You see what comes of letting the South Side go to hell! This pair comes stumbling in here, pouring blood. I knew one of them—

the trail boss, name of Walker. He tried to give me his gun, but I told him, 'It's too late for that. Throw it on the floor if you don't want it.' Is it true they shot Ed Masterson? Damn! He's a good man, but maybe a little too easygoing for this job!"

"He was still alive when I left him," Channing said, "but I don't give him much of a chance."

Afterward, he turned to have a look at the pair Masterson had shot it out with—it was now that he recognized one of them—the man he had known by the name of Jim Fitch.

Ed Masterson lived for half an hour, never regaining consciousness, with his brother Bat close by him until the end. Afterward, the sheriff lost no time getting warrants sworn for the rest of the half dozen who had created a disturbance at the Lady Gay; he went out and collected them, and within an hour of the shooting they were all in jail. It seemed unlikely they would stay there, with no evidence that any of them had taken any actual part in shooting Dodge City's marshal.

And though Burl Channing went to have a look at them, he couldn't tell if they included the pair who had helped Jim Fitch waylay him that night outside Ham Bell's livery; probably no one would ever know if the marshal's shooting had somehow stemmed from that other incident. Fitch and the trail boss, Alf Walker, had been moved to a room over Wright & Beverley's store where they could be kept under the doctor's surveillance. There seemed little chance either man would live or, even if they did, that Jim Fitch could tell anything about Killian's whereabouts.

Yet Fitch was Channing's only glimmer of a lead; so

155

far, Wes Lowe's suggestion concerning hunting out high-stakes private games had produced nothing. Doc Clevenger offered little hope. "There's no way this man can survive the wound he took from Masterson," the doctor said. "He barely got through the night; he won't last out the day. And I can't see him finding strength enough to talk."

"I'll be around just the same," Channing said grimly.

Dodge City had begun a day of deep mourning. By ten, every business house was closed, its doorway draped in black. Ed Masterson's funeral was scheduled for that afternoon. It promised to be a big one. Bob Wright, whom Channing met in front of his store, summed it up as well as anyone: "The town respects Bat Masterson, but the feeling for his brother was a little different. Ed was a gentle-hearted man—it ain't too much to say that everybody loved him. He won't be easy to replace. We might get Wyatt Earp in here for the job or even that other Masterson boy—Jim; he has a good reputation. But it's a sad, sad thing!"

"What time is the funeral?"

"Two o'clock—in the military cemetery at the fort. I wager the whole town will be there. Boot Hill is good enough for the man who killed him but not for our marshal!"

Channing was on the porch of the Dodge House when the funeral cortege pulled out of Dodge City. It was a long one, and impressive; almost every buggy and wagon in town seemed to be involved. The members of the city council rode ahead of the hearse, and just behind it the dead marshal's brother, Bat, sat alone in his light rig. After him followed, in uniform, the sixty members of the volunteer fire department—Ed had been one of them—

156

and then came the long tail of vehicles containing the marshal's many friends and mourners.

Channing stood with hat in hand watching the silent procession move out of sight, eastward alongside the bright steel of the railroad embankment. He had some slow thoughts that were broken presently as Emily Barker spoke. "You aren't going?"

He turned in some surprise; he'd thought he was alone, but she had come out quietly and stood almost at his elbow without him being aware of her. He answered, "I'd have liked to. Ed Masterson was a good man. But I don't think I should leave."

"Then you believe Frank Killian is still somewhere here in Dodge?"

"I'm finding it harder all the time to be sure," he admitted. Then, in a way that was not at all like him, he found himself pouring out his frustrations to her. "Why hasn't he made a move? Where could he be holed up? Why haven't I been able to ferret him out?" He indicated the spread of boxlike wooden buildings, most of them no more than a single story, that made up Dodge City. He shook his head. "It has me licked!"

Emily was looking at him with an odd expression. The last of the funeral cortege for Ed Masterson was nearly gone now, the slow creak of timbers and grind of wheels and plodding of hoofs dwindling to stillness. A rooster crowed somewhere in the silence of the sun-warmed afternoon. "Do you realize," she said slowly, "that for almost the first time, you and I are actually talking together—friendly and honest, neither of us keeping up a guard!"

Channing saw the smile that lurked in her eyes. At once, he felt an easing in his own stiffness and reserve. "It is sort of pleasant, isn't it. Our trouble all seemed to begin on that stagecoach when you pegged me for the killer in McAfee's letter. After that, I guess there wasn't a chance of you seeing me as anything else."

Emily nodded soberly. "And of course you had no way of knowing why I should be acting the way I did. It's a wonder now you even so much as speak to me!"

"On the other hand," he pointed out, "you haven't made it a secret that you don't really approve of me. The work I do—my being connected with Judge Parker—"

"Oh."

They were silent a moment. She had turned away, and Channing could see only the brown of her hair sweeping back over one delicate ear. But from the set of her shoulders, somehow he got an impression that she was working with troubling thoughts and with words that didn't come easily. She lifted her eyes to his then, and it was with an earnest frown that she said in a swift rush, "You see, I didn't understand—not till you told me something of the job you have facing you down there in Indian territory. I see now that it's a job that has to be done. I've given a lot of thought to what you told me. And I want you to know how very wrong I have been. I'm sure now you're a very fine person, Burl Channing. Otherwise, you wouldn't have pledged yourself to finding the one who murdered your friend." And as he stared at her, all speech knocked out of him by what she was saying, Emily put her hand on his and let it rest there a moment as she said earnestly, "There—does that help at all to make amends?"

She turned and went back into the hotel, not waiting for an answer.

* * *

Channing was mounting the outside stairs to the room above Wright & Beverley's when the door at the top opened and Doc Clevenger appeared, bag in hand. From the man's expression, Channing knew what he was going to say before he said it: "You're too late. Your man's gone."

"Did he—?"

"Say anything? Not a word. He was in shock and never came out of it."

"I see." He had to take the news in stride. It had been a very long shot that a man, wounded as Jim Fitch had been, would ever be able to answer any questions—assuming that he'd even known of Frank Killian's present whereabouts or could be persuaded to tell. This was another door slammed shut. As Channing halted in front of Wright's and watched the doctor hurry off along the street, he experienced a letdown and with it a growing doubt.

It really began to look as though his string had played out, that he might not accomplish the urgent mission that had brought him to Dodge City. He wasn't a man for whom failure came easily. This one gave him the empty feeling of owing a debt to the memory of Tom Nolan—a debt that was going unpaid.

He was so deep in these thoughts that he scarcely heard the sound of his own name. Now it was repeated: "Channing!" He turned to find Cora Tyler beside him there beneath the store awning, with the black-draped door beside them. She seemed breathless—whether from hurry or under some kind of emotional excitement. The warm day had put a faint sheen of perspiration over her carefully groomed features.

Surprised, he asked, "Can I do something for you?"

159

"You can do something for both of us," she answered with her usual abrupt manner. "I've found out where he is."

He looked at her sharply. "Killian?"

"I can take you right to him whenever you say." Then, seeing his grim expression, she demanded, "What's wrong? I guess you don't trust me, do you? You think this is some kind of trick!"

Channing shook his head. "I trust you," he assured her. "But I wonder if you can trust yourself! Are you sure this is what you really want to do? Because once you've told me, it's going to be too late to change your mind. You know I intend to take him—whatever that involves."

"You're thinking I could still give a damn about what happens to the sonofabitch?" she retorted, and anger turned her attractive face almost ugly. She made an impatient gesture. "Once my eyes have been opened, mister, they stay that way! There's no way he'd ever pull the wool over them again!"

"All right, Cora," he said. "I just wanted that settled; where's Killian? You've seen him?"

"I know somebody who has. I got a friend that works in one of those houses on the South Side."

Channing stared at her. "You mean *that's* where he is? In a whorehouse?"

"Aunt Sadie's. Maybe he has something on her—or maybe she just fell for his line, like some other saps I know of! Anyway, Sadie's put him up, and she told her girls she'd personally break the neck of any one of them that squealed. But this friend of mine doesn't give a damn about Sadie. And she knew I'd be interested."

So he had his answer—and it was not one that would ever have suggested itself to him. No private games for

Frank Killian; just a whorehouse madam sweet-talked or threatened into hiding him! Burl Channing settled his shoulders. He said roughly, "Where's Sadie's?"

"Come with me," Cora told him.

Chapter 14

Much of the red-light district consisted of squalid little huts occupied by the girls of the "line," but there were a few solid-looking houses, and Sadie's was one of the biggest. A sprawling, two-story wooden building, it boasted a recent coat of whitewash and even had a few purple and orange crocuses poking up in flower beds that were probably tended by Sadie's charges in their off hours. Cora Tyler, having brought Channing to the rear of the place, left him to watch from a nearby shed while she crossed the barren yard that held a scatter of junk and cast-off, broken furniture.

Her prostitute friend must have been on the lookout for her because the door opened before she reached it. There was a brief conference, and then Cora was signaling Channing in. "This is Jill," she said by way of introduction.

Jill, a thin girl with raddled features and arms like pipe stems, clutched her dressing gown about her. She was trembling with nervousness. When Channing demanded, "Well, where is he?" she hesitated and gave Cora a questioning look.

"It's all right," Cora said. Still clearly unconvinced, Jill checked the hallway and then, without a word, opened the door just wide enough for Channing to enter; Cora remained outside. The hall, dark and deserted, held the stale smells of cooking and perfume; an occasional squabbling of women's voices could be heard upstairs. Channing followed the girl up a flight of steps to the second floor. He was beginning to wonder just what he was letting himself in for. At the top of the stairs was another corridor—shadowed and deserted. The girl stopped at one of the doors that lined it and looked at Channing.

"He's in there?" he said.

His own voice seemed suddenly very loud in the stillness; Jill shot a look around her, anxiety in every line of her pinched features. She whispered tremulously, "He never goes out. But please! If Sadie ever finds out it was me that told—she'll just skin me *alive*!"

Channing nodded. She thanked him with a frightened smile and then turned and left him there, making quickly for the stairs. He watched her go and afterward turned to the door.

He listened for something to tell him Killian was in there and whether or not he was alone. No sound came through the flimsy partition; tense now and growing impatient, he put a hand on the knob and gently tried it. The door was unlocked. He drew his gun and nudged the door wide.

For a moment, he thought the room was empty. The blinds had been drawn, and it was in semidarkness; there was no movement, nothing but his own breathing and a stale smell of dust and bodies, whiskey and cheap perfume. But now he saw the figure sprawled on the unmade bed; he closed the door and went over to stand looking down at Frank Killian.

The man was on his back, asleep, fully dressed even to his shoes. He had changed so much Channing might have failed to recognize him. There was little resemblance to the smooth and carefully dressed faro dealer he had encountered in the Long Branch. His clothes were rumpled, his features slack and darkened by a scraggly growth of unshaven whiskers. A reek of whiskey came from him and from the half-empty bottle that stood open on a table by the bed. It suddenly occurred to Channing that here, at last, was the Frank Killian who had been described to him at North Platte as a down-and-out tinhorn gambler—the one he had come to Dodge expecting to find.

Come full circle!

He placed the muzzle of his gun against the side of the man's throat. For a moment, there was no reaction; then the breathing that fluttered Killian's slack lips choked off, started again. The man's eyes shot open; they stared into Channing's face and suddenly flooded with terror. He stiffened, and a babble of incoherent words rushed and died as Channing pressed the muzzle harder. "Careful!" Channing warned.

A groan broke from his prisoner. "How did you find me?" Killian demanded hoarsely. "What are you, Channing—a damned bloodhound?"

"Bulldog," Channing corrected him dryly. "One that hangs on and doesn't know enough to quit!" He saw the man's shoulder rig hanging from a bed knob. He lifted the gun out of its holster, shoved it behind his waist belt, and then stepped back with his own weapon ready.

"Get up!" he ordered.

Frank Killian rolled over, swung his legs off the bed, and sat up. He looked sick. He started to reach for the

164

whiskey, but Burl Channing moved it away, saying, "Haven't you had enough of this already?" The man glared at him but let him have the bottle. Channing replaced it on the table and, looking down at the gambler, said with a shake of the head, "You've gone quite a long way down the hill since I saw you last."

"Go to hell!"

Channing knew the answer to his own question. Too much had gone wrong in too short a time for someone as unstable as Killian—someone bound up as he was with superstition. Being persuaded that Emily Barker and this town of Dodge constituted his "luck," it was more than he could bear to see her turn from him and to be closed out of the Long Branch all within the space of an hour. Channing remembered something Tug Wheeler, the stage driver, had said about gamblers as a breed: *If they figure their luck is in, then they're ten feet tall; but once it sets against 'em, they crumble to nothing.* So it was now with Frank Killian.

"All right," Channing said crisply, "I'll tell you what you're going to do. You're going to come along with me, and you're not going to make me any trouble at all. If we run into Aunt Sadie on our way out, you'll thank her for her hospitality and tell her you're leaving. But—no fuss. Remember that!"

The gambler raised his head and looked at the gun pointed at him. "I'm to go quiet," he said heavily, "so you can take me off someplace and murder me!"

"Murder?" Channing echoed. His jaw set grimly. "Don't tempt me!"

He found the man's hat and coat on a chair; there seemed nothing else in the room that could have been his. Killian put the hat on and hung the coat over an arm. A

165

glance into the hall showed it empty, and Channing motioned the other man out, ahead of him.

As they headed for the rear stairs, a sudden screech of harpy laughter echoed somewhere in the building. They went down the back stairs without encountering anyone and gained the rear doorway by which Channing had entered. They stepped outside into the cluttered yard. There was no sign of Cora; she had apparently chosen to make herself scarce.

"This way," Channing ordered. He marched his prisoner through the alley, following with his gun in its holster but his hand resting on it in case the man gave any trouble. But there didn't seem to be any trouble in him. Killian went doggedly, all the fight seemingly drained from him. At the alley entrance, Channing pointed him toward Front Street, along one of the streets that led up from the South Side.

They had gone only a few steps when Killian suddenly balked, turning on his captor and exclaiming: "Damn you! I got a right to know where you're taking me."

Channing told him. "There should be a stage out of here tomorrow or next day. We're going to be on it. We're heading for North Platte where you'll tell the authorities everything you know about the murder of Tom Nolan."

Too quickly, Killian protested. "I never killed him. I don't know anything about it!"

"Well, then, you've got nothing to worry about, *have* you?"

"You think I believe that? I know you're lying! You just want me to keep quiet until it's convenient to kill me and put me out of the way."

Burl Channing found his patience slipping. "It's twice now you've accused me of that."

"I know it's true. I had warning!"

Channing looked at him. "That letter from McAfee? I'm curious as hell. Just what did he tell you?"

"Enough! That you were sure I was the one killed your friend. That you'd sworn to shoot me down like a dog!"

Channing could only stare. "He's lying. All I said to McAfee was that I figured you knew something about the murder and that I was going to get it out of you. Nothing about killing you."

The gambler's face turned slowly red. "Why the sonofabitch!" he exclaimed hoarsely. "So that's his game!" He gave a bitter laugh. "Smart bastard, that McAfee—"

"What do you mean?"

Frank Killian said, "McAfee murdered Nolan! He did it for that money belt—"

"You expect me to believe that? McAfee's a businessman. He already owns half of North Platte!"

"His kind never has enough."

Killian turned away. Burl Channing swore and seized the gambler, hauling him around and slamming him hard against a shed. "All right, Killian!" He fought to control a turmoil of emotions. "I want the rest—and you better be convincing!"

The gambler quailed and began to stammer. "Man, I can only tell you what happened! I swear, I never did Nolan any harm. I swear—that night the two of us met up in a bar, and he seemed to take a liking to me. I was flat broke, and—well, he had cash and seemed willing to spend it. But I never knew there was a money belt on him!

I'm no killer! You've got to believe me! If I was, I'd have done for you that first day you came!"

Channing said tightly, "Go on! Where does Jared McAfee fit into this?"

"He knew about the money belt. The thought of all that cash drove him crazy. He must have followed us all evening, waiting for his chance. And it came when Nolan and I got separated for a minute—I think the fellow stepped into an alley to take a leak. At any rate, I missed him and went back to look, and there he was lying on the cinders with blood on his head. And McAfee was just pulling the belt loose."

Channing said contemptuously, "You're spinning a good yarn—"

"It's the truth, I tell you! Every word!" There was sweat on Killian's forehead and in the unshaven stubble of his cheeks. "I swear it!" To give emphasis, he made an anxious grab at Channing's arm, but the lawman shook his hand away.

"So naturally," Channing supplied in a note of sarcasm, "you went to the marshal and had Jared McAfee arrested for murder!"

"You know damn well I didn't!" the gambler cried. "Who would have believed me—my word against a big man like him?"

"But he couldn't be absolutely sure you wouldn't? So now you're going to tell me he made a deal to buy you off and keep you quiet. How much did he offer you?"

The gambler's mouth worked crookedly. "Five thousand."

"Out of twenty-five? You should have held out for half."

"Damn it, I took what I could get! I bought a horse

168

that night and got out of town—just in case he had it in mind to pin the murder on me. I kept going and didn't stop until I hit Dodge."

"Where you used that money of Tom Nolan's to finance your faro game. . . ."

"And my luck's been good," Killian shot back, "until you came along!" Pure hatred mingled with anguish in Frank Killian's expression.

For a long moment, Burl Channing was silent, thinking over what he had heard. They stood there in the empty alley. A glow of sunset touched the ugly rawness of the town with a golden light. Channing said finally, "It must have come as a real surprise to get a letter from McAfee that I was after you."

"I didn't know why in hell he would bother," Killian admitted. "But now I understand. He's more scared of you than he ever was of me. But he figured if I had enough warning, I'd get rid of you for him."

"Or if we did each other in, he'd be rid of us both. It's not a bad yarn, Killian."

The other man stared at him. "Then—you *believe* me?"

"For now it makes a kind of sense. But I'm still hauling you back to North Platte and confronting McAfee with it."

"With no more than my word to back it?" He grunted hopelessly. "You'll never pin it on him, Channing. You'll just get me hanged!"

"That's your gamble."

A distant sound lifted Channing's head. From where he stood, he could look north across the Plaza and see the stage road that led into Front Street and Dodge. There, just swelling into view, a coach and four-horse hitch raised a plume of dust in a rhythm of pounding hoofs. The low sun gilded the dust and picked glints of brightness from harness metal and spinning wheels. " When the stage heads north, we'll be on it—if I have to tie you hand and foot to do it. You'd better make up your mind to that! "

Chapter 15

The arrival of a coach at the depot across the street brought Emily to her window. She watched the horses pull up in the traces and the coach rocked to a halt. The stage looked like the same trail-scarred rig that had brought her to Dodge just a week ago. She recognized Tug Wheeler's stocky figure on the box as he tromped the brake and issued his standard call to his passengers: "Dodge City, folks—end of the line. Accommodations across the street at the Dodge House, on your right."

The same streak of curiosity that brought idlers to the station to see coaches and trains arrive held Emily where she was, watching from her window as the driver swung down off his perch to unfasten the leather shield of the luggage boot. The coach door opened, and passengers began to climb down one by one. In surprise, she recognized somebody she knew—there could be no mistaking the neat, spare frame, the lean face with its graying sideburns. He took the awkward drop from the iron step with agility for a man accustomed to spending his life behind a desk. Emily said aloud, "Mister McAfee!"

Given the scope of Jared McAfee's business enterprises, any number of reasons could bring him this far afield; all the same, her former employer was the last person Emily expected at that moment. There was pleasure in seeing a familiar face; she turned away from the window, determined to go down at once and greet him.

Wes Lowe had also watched Jared McAfee alight from the stage; the gun fighter unfolded his lean frame from a chair on the porch of the Dodge House and, unhurrying, descended to the street. McAfee, absently brushing dust from his clothing, glanced up and saw the gunman. At once, his eyes went hard. Without preliminary, Wes Lowe told him, "Thought you might show up."

"I was certain to," McAfee said in a tone of stern displeasure, "once I got your wire about the state of things here. I had no choice but to come and try to straighten out this mess you've made."

The gunman's eyes flickered, a warning of anger. "I don't take kindly to that!"

"No other way to put it, Lowe," McAfee retorted; he showed no sign of being intimidated. Standing there amid the bustle of activity around the coach, he kept his voice down, but it was heavy with angry scorn. "I paid you to do a job you shouldn't have had any trouble doing—it was all set up for you with that letter I sent Killian. You were supposed to be there when they went at it! You weren't, and they both walked away." McAfee glared at Lowe. "I paid you well to see that they both went down for good."

"Your plan didn't work," Lowe said coldly, "because it was bad to begin with. Too many things went wrong. Just before the stage got us into Dodge, a couple of amateurs tried a holdup, and I had to shoot one. On account of it, Bat Masterson insisted on a statement; that kept me from being on hand when Killian made his first try at Channing—and failed. There hasn't been another chance since."

McAfee was not mollified. "That's not good enough!

We have got to do something and do it fast. Because as long as those two are alive, there's too good a chance the Nolan killing will be traced back to me and—" He broke off in midsentence, seeing the direction of the other man's stare. Something in the look warned McAfee. He turned to find Emily Barker standing within earshot.

Jared McAfee recovered quickly. "Why, my dear!" he exclaimed, feigning pleased surprise. "You still in Dodge? I thought you'd be home in Missouri long before this."

But there was no answer. Emily stood looking at him with a pallor in her cheeks and all the appearance of someone in shock. McAfee dropped the pretense, but his tone was still mild as he said reproachfully, "I'm very much afraid you've been listening. You heard what I was saying just now, didn't you?"

She found her voice. "I heard enough! *You* killed Tom Nolan. Frank Killian knew, and *that* was your obligation to him!" The word "obligation," as she spoke it, had all the bitterness of a rebuke. "And you used me—to set a trap for Burl Channing. . . ."

"Now, now!" McAfee worried the inside of a lip as he glanced quickly about, lest strangers might be showing too much interest. He chided her: "We mustn't have a scene here in public—*must* we? I assure you that you've misunderstood. Why don't we just step off the street, find someplace where we can talk this over, and straighten out whatever's troubling you?" He smiled again and took her firmly by the arm.

"No!" She tried to pull free, but his grip was too strong. "*Let me alone!*"

The smile vanished. McAfee's hold tightened. "Are you determined to make trouble?"

She struck at him, really struggling now. And it was

at this moment that Burl Channing, with Frank Killian in tow, came across the slight embankment crowned by the Santa Fe tracks and saw them.

"McAfee! Damn you, let go of her!"

Startled, McAfee turned. Emily had her chance and was able to break free, moving quickly out of reach. Killian balked at sight of the enemy who had frightened him out of Nebraska, but Channing shoved the gambler ahead of him, and Jared McAfee stood and watched them come. Lowe moved to one side.

Emily cried, "Burl! Watch out for Lowe—" At almost the same instant, the gunfighter's hand flashed to his pistol. Channing stopped in his tracks and half turned, with the instinct to make himself a smaller target.

It all broke apart then.

Channing quickly sidestepped, and the shot Wes Lowe flung at him missed. His own gun banged, but the confusion around the stagecoach, the danger to Emily and to the bystanders, hampered his aim and made him pull high. An instant later, cinders gouged up near his boot by a second bullet from Wes Lowe's revolver.

The roar of gunfire had brought chaos. Men in the street scattered like quail, yelling; and the stage horses, terror stricken, exploded, squealing and rearing in their harness. Big Tug Wheeler hurled himself at his team, unmindful of the danger from bullets or from having his skull mashed by a steel-shod hoof as he tried to grab the leaders' headstalls and settle them with curses and the weight of his own body.

Jared McAfee and Wes Lowe held their ground. McAfee had produced a gun from someplace, and he threw a shot, but by now Channing was bolting in a crouch for a corner of the station building. Channing fired back on the run, and a bullet from Wes Lowe chewed a long sliver of wood from the building's corner as he ducked behind it. The frightened stage teams surged forward, dragging the heavy coach between Channing and his enemies, and for the moment he no longer had a target.

Frank Killian, who had first made a move to follow, changed his mind. Apparently, the gambler thought he saw a chance for freedom. He turned and made a dash for the Santa Fe tracks, where he went scrambling up the low embankment of the right of way. Channing yelled something after him, but it was already too late; Killian had reached the crown and was a step from safety when a bullet from McAfee's pistol caught him and chopped him down. His knees buckled, and he twisted about and fell in a loose sprawl, to slide back down the graded embankment and lie limp and unmoving at the foot of it.

Burl Channing swore as he saw that. He was crouched tensely, trying to get a look between the legs of the horses and through the dust they raised. That proving impossible, he left his place and set off along the station platform toward the rear of the stagecoach. He reached it and swung wide around the luggage boot, whose unfastened leather shield flapped loosely to the wild rocking of the coach. And he came face to face with both his enemies.

They had guessed his maneuver. They were waiting for him. But before McAfee could shoot, Emily Barker hurled herself at him with furious blows and kicks, distracting him and leaving Channing with Wes Lowe. The two men looked at each other, neither moving; and Channing had time for a silent protest.

This was a man he would never understand but one he had come to respect and, almost, to like—and a man

175

who, he would almost have sworn, liked him in return. But the gunman followed his own code; when he hired out to kill a man, he delivered the goods he had been paid for despite possible friendship. They both fired in almost the same instant, the reports mingling. Untouched, Channing watched the other man stumble, then break and fall.

At the same moment, Jared McAfee had rid himself of Emily; Channing caught a glimpse of her lying in the street where the man had flung her. Then McAfee's gun spurted flame and a blow struck Channing, whirling him around and slamming him against the side of the stagecoach. The gun flew from his hand, struck the iron step with a clang, and bounced away. The whole upper part of his body went numb.

But he was still on his feet, and he remembered Frank Killian's snub-nosed gun shoved behind his belt. He groped for it, expecting the next bullet from McAfee that would finish him. Then he heard the shot but strangely didn't feel any impact—it was simply weakness that dropped him to his knees, catching at the iron coach step to keep from going face down in the dust. Through a throb of pain, as the wound in his shoulder began to thaw, he stared across the dust of Front Street and saw why Jared McAfee hadn't finished the job of killing him.

McAfee was down, desperately clutching a bleeding leg; above him, Bat Masterson stood with smoke rising from the muzzle of the revolver with which he'd fired that last shot. Nearby stood the rig in which the sheriff had ridden back from his brother's burial at the fort.

After that, everything else was blocked away as Emily Barker bent over him. Concentrating, Channing looked up into her anxious face. It was chalk white and streaked with dirt and tears. He felt he had to reassure her;

he heard himself saying, "No need for you to cry. It's over. You're safe now."

"Me?" she said, and her mouth trembled. "Oh, damn you, Burl Channing! Can't you see it's you I'm crying about?"

Another dawn was breaking over Dodge, first light spreading along the flat horizon; lamps that still burned in the Santa Fe depot and in a few other places along Front Street were dimmed with the brightening of day. It was one of the few times of the day when the town was completely still. Burl Channing sat on a bench under the overhang of the depot roof and worked at a cigar, savoring the quiet. He gently rubbed his right arm, hanging in the sling Doc Clevenger had fashioned.

When a solitary figure left the Dodge House and came toward him across Front Street, he tossed his cigar away as he got quickly to his feet. Emily Barker was wearing her traveling coat and carrying her bag and reticule. She nodded and smiled "Good morning" as she set the bag down.

It seemed to him her smile was a shade too bright, her cheerful greeting forced—as though she had steeled herself against some ordeal. Frowning, he exclaimed, "What are you up to?"

"How is the arm?" she asked as though she hadn't heard.

"What? Not too bad," he said, moving it slightly within its sling and not letting her see him wince. "Clevenger must have been right when he said luck was with me. He told me it would be sore for a while but nothing worse than that—in the long run, probably not even a stiff shoulder."

"But are you sure it isn't too sore for another long stage trip?"

"Not this one!" he told her, and with grim satisfaction showed her the paper he carried in his pocket.

It was Frank Killian's sworn statement, notarized and witnessed by both Bat Masterson and the judge who had taken it, charging Jared McAfee with the murder of Tom Nolan. As a result of the shootout the evening before last, Killian and McAfee lay in adjoining cells of the Ford County jail, pouring out mutual hatred while they recovered from bullet wounds. For now, Channing hoped this paper would be enough for the authorities in North Platte to arrange extradition and a trial.

"I think it's the ammunition I need," he said. "At least it should start the machinery turning that will see McAfee convicted," he said. "Perhaps even get Maude Nolan back her twenty-five thousand dollars." After a moment, he added, "But you haven't answered *my* question. I know it's none of my business, but I'd still like to know where you're off to."

Her head lifted, and on a note of defiance she said, "Why to the same place you are! You haven't forgotten that I'm a witness? I heard with my own ears Jared McAfee say he'd murdered Tom Nolan. Shouldn't that make a difference?"

"It should make all the difference in the world," Channing agreed. "But Emily! I can't have you—"

"Just the same, I'm going! I'm hoping it's one way I can help make it up to you for all the wrong things I thought and did—so don't tell me I can't! And besides—" She hesitated, as though her confidence threatened to fail her; then it came out, all in a rush: "Besides, if you leave on that stage and I don't go with you . . . then I don't suppose we'll ever see each other again!"

He said slowly, "Is that important to you?"

"Isn't it to you?"

The warmth of the look he gave her broke the dark gravity of his face. "Almost from the moment we met, at that stage station in Nebraska," he told her, "I've tried not to let myself admit just how important it really is!"

He spoke her name, and it seemed only natural then that she should move into the circle of his uninjured arm and that their lips should meet. After a moment, Burl Channing said gruffly, "You'd better know something about me. I'm not going to give up carrying this U.S. marshal's badge as long as I think there's still a job I can do. . . ."

Emily placed a finger upon his lips. "Please! Don't waste your breath trying to talk me out of it!"

They kissed again, sharing the wonder of the love they had found, as a rising sun began to pour new warmth and color over the drab roughness of Front Street. And now the morning stage came rolling toward them, the horses restive and high-spirited; and Channing lifted a hand in greeting to red-bearded Tug Wheeler, grinning down at them from the driver's seat.

"Couple of passengers for you," Channing said.

"Care to ride on the box with me again?" Wheeler jumped down. "I'd admire to have your company— breaks the boredom of things."

Burl Channing shook his head as he helped Emily into the coach. "Thanks—but not this time."

As Channing moved to climb into the coach, Wheeler looked past him at the young woman and indulged in a knowing grin. "Well, I guess you don't have to worry about boredom!" He slammed the door shut. "Let's roll, then!"

Tug Wheeler climbed to his seat, shook out his lines,

and shouted his teams into an eager, lunging start on the long road from Dodge City.

"The *Stagecoach* series is great frontier entertainment. Hank Mitchum really makes the West come alive in each story."

—Dana Fuller Ross, author of *Wagons West*

STAGECOACH STATION II:

HANK MITCHUM

At high noon the dusty border pueblo of Laredo would be charged with excitement. The wily curly wolf of an outlaw, Bart Campion—a legend along the Rio Grande—had finally been caught and was about to be hung for murder. Spectators from all over the rugged spine of Texas and beyond filled the Laredo-bound stages to bursting, including vulnerable eighteen-year-old Molly Bishop, desperate to have Bart reveal the answer to the question that has shadowed her entire life before he dies. For help she turns to the strong young rancher Owen Pryor who has his own dark score from the past to settle with Bart and his gang.

Buy LAREDO at your local bookstore or use this handy coupon for ordering:

Bantam Books, Inc., Dept. SC2, 414 East Golf Road, Des Plaines, Ill. 60016

Please send me _____ copies of LAREDO (14985-7 • $2.25). I am enclosing $_____ (please add $1.25 to cover postage and handling, send check or money order—no cash or C.O.D.'s please).

Mr/Mrs/Miss_____

Address_____

City_____ State/Zip _____

SC2—10/82

Please allow four to six weeks for delivery. This offer expires 4/83.

★★★★★★★★★★★★★★★★★★★★★★★

GREAT HISTORICAL SAGAS OF AMERICA'S FIRST FRONTIERS

The Producer of the KENT FAMILY CHRONICLES now brings you the WAGONS WEST and COLONIZATION OF AMERICA series. These books are full of the spectacular adventure and romance that followed America's first settlers as they struggled in a new land.

The highly acclaimed WAGONS WEST series by Dana Fuller Ross:

☐	22803	INDEPENDENCE!	$3.50
☐	22784	NEBRASKA!	$3.50
☐	20420	WYOMING!	$3.25
☐	22568	OREGON!	$3.50
☐	20422	TEXAS!	$3.25
☐	14260	CALIFORNIA!	$2.95
☐	14717	COLORADO!	$3.25
☐	20174	NEVADA!	$3.50
☐	20919	WASHINGTON!	$3.50

The thrilling COLONIZATION OF AMERICA series by Donald Clayton Porter:

☐	20349	WHITE INDIAN	$3.25
☐	22715	THE RENEGADE	$3.50
☐	20579	WAR CHIEF	$3.25
☐	20361	THE SACHEM	$3.25
☐	20028	RENNO	$3.25
☐	20559	TOMAHAWK	$3.50

The new SAGA OF THE SOUTHWEST series by Leigh Franklin James

☐	20556	HAWK OF THE DOVE	$3.25
☐	20635	WINGS OF THE HAWK	$3.25
☐	20096	REVENGE OF THE HAWK	$3.25

★★★★★★★★★★★★★★★★★★★★★★★

Buy them at your local bookstore or use this handy coupon:

Bantam Books, Inc., Dept. LE, 414 East Golf Road, Des Plaines, Ill. 60016

Please send me the books I have checked above. I am enclosing $_____ (please add $1.25 to cover postage and handling). Send check or money order —no cash or C.O.D.'s please.

Mr/Mrs/Miss _____

Address _____

City _____ State/Zip _____

LE—10/82

Please allow four to six weeks for delivery. This offer expires 4/83.

FROM THE PRODUCER OF WAGONS WEST AND THE KENT FAMILY CHRONICLES— A SWEEPING SAGA OF WAR AND HEROISM AT THE BIRTH OF A NATION.

THE WHITE INDIAN SERIES

Filled with the glory and adventure of the colonization of America, here is the thrilling saga of one of the new frontier's boldest heroes. He is Renno, born to white parents, raised by Seneca Indians, and destined to be a leader in both worlds. THE WHITE INDIAN SERIES chronicles Renno's adventures from the colonies to Canada, from the South to the turbulent West. Through Renno's struggles to tame a savage continent and through his encounters with the powerful men and passionate women on all sides of the early battles of America, we witness the events that shaped our future and forged our great heritage.

☐	20349	White Indian #1	$3.25
☐	22715	The Renegade #2	$3.50
☐	20579	War Chief #3	$3.25
☐	20361	The Sachem #4	$3.25
☐	20028	Renno #5	$3.25
☐	20559	Tomahawk #6	$3.50

Bantam Books, Inc., Dept. LE3, 414 East Golf Road, Des Plaines, Ill. 60016

Please send me the books I have checked above. I am enclosing
$_____ (please add $1.25 to cover postage and handling). Send check or money order—no cash or C.O.D.'s please.

Mr/Mrs/Miss _____

Address _____

City _____ State/Zip _____

LE3-10/82

Please allow four to six weeks for delivery. This offer expires 4/83.

☐ **TEXAS! BOOK V** (20422)
1843. The fledgling republic fights for its life against the onrush of Mexican soldiers. Some of the original wagon train members join the call to help in this struggle. **$3.25**

☐ **CALIFORNIA! BOOK VI** (14260)
Gold is discovered in 1848 and its lure attracts friend and foe alike... in a mad scramble for new-found riches. But many lives become endangered as lawlessness overtakes the territory. **$2.95**

☐ **COLORADO! BOOK VII** (14717)
Now gold is found in Central City, and the frontier town of Denver becomes the magnet for hucksters, and many of the wagon train friends. Shocking events result from this highly volatile situation. **$3.25**

☐ **NEVADA! BOOK VIII** (20174)
In the midst of a Civil War, Major General Lee Blake is summoned to spearhead a mission of utmost importance to the Union cause. Aided by his long-time friend and wagon master, Whip Holt, Whip's courageous son, a beautiful, sharp-shooting newswoman and a seductive courtesan, the vital journey begins. **$3.50**

☐ **WASHINGTON! BOOK IX** (20919)
Now it is the close of the Civil War. Wounded hero, Toby Hall, returns from battle and rides West to claim a homestead on the vast timberlands of WASHINGTON! Awaiting him are ruthless profiteers enticed by the promise of fabulous wealth and bent on robbing Toby of his land's riches. **$3.50**

Bantam Books, Inc., Dept. LE2, 414 East Golf Road, Des Plaines, Ill. 60016

Please send me the books I have checked above. I am enclosing $_____ (please add $1.25 to cover postage and handling). Send check or money order —no cash or C.O.D.'s please.

Mr/Mrs/Miss_____

Address_____

City_____ State/Zip_____

LE2—10/82

Please allow four to six weeks for delivery. This offer expires 4/83.